Ask Lily

Other Books Available

The Lily Series

Here's Lily!
Lily Robbins, M.D. (Medical Dabbler)
Lily and the Creep
Lily's Ultimate Party
Ask Lily
Lily the Rebel
Lights, Action, Lily!
Lily Rules!
Rough & Rugged Lily
Lily Speaks!
Horse Crazy Lily
Lily's Church Camp Adventure
Lily's in London?!
Lily's Passport to Paris

Nonfiction

The Beauty Book
The Body Book
The Buddy Book
The Best Bash Book
The Blurry Rules Book
The It's MY Life Book
The Creativity Book
The Uniquely Me Book
The Values & Virtues Book
The Year 'Round Holiday Book
The Fun-Finder Book
The Walk-the-Walk Book
NIV Young Women of Faith Bible

Ask Lily

Nancy Rue

zonderkidz

ZONDERVAN.com/
AUTHORTRACKER
follow your favorite authors

www.zonderkidz.com

Ask Lily

Requests for information should be addressed to:
Zonderkidz, Grand Rapids, Michigan 49530

ISBN-13: 978-0-310-23254-4
ISBN-10: 0-310-23254-6

Published in association with the literary agency of Alive Communications, Inc., 7680 Goddard Street, Suite 200, Colorado Springs, CO 80920.
www.alivecommunications.com

Cover design: Jody Langley
Interior design: Amy Lengler

Printed in the United States of America

07 08 09 10 11 12 • 21 20 19 18 17 16

Lily, come on! We're gonna be late!"

"I can't get this stupid locker open!"

"We're gonna get in trouble—you heard what Mrs. Reinhold said—"

Lily blew her mop of red hair out of her face and attacked the lock again. "Yeah, Reni," she said. "If we come to class without our literature books we're chopped meat. Do you remember my combination?"

"I can't even remember mine!" Reni glanced over her shoulder at the last of the kids streaming out of the locker area toward their classrooms. "We're gonna get busted for being late, and Mr. Lamb's gonna hear about it, and that's gonna go against me making All-State Orchestra."

Lily gave the lock another vicious twist, and the locker door popped open. *Adventures in World Literature* tumbled out onto her foot.

Reni snatched it up and made off for D–104. Still wincing, Lily slammed the locker door, slung her backpack (which was still gaping open) over her shoulder, and limped after Reni.

You're going to like middle school so much more than elementary, Lily, Ms. Gooch, her sixth-grade teacher, had told her at the end of last year.

"Oh, yeah, I adore it," she muttered to herself as she hobbled the last few steps to her classroom. There were two different locker combinations to remember—PE *and* a book locker—and seven different teachers' rules to follow, *plus* the nine hundred rules Cedar Hills Middle School had on its list.

Even now, she realized she was walking on the wrong side of the hallway, and she had to swerve abruptly to get back to where she was supposed to be. Bad move. Three binders escaped from the unzipped backpack and dumped themselves and their contents in an arc across the floor. Last night's English homework made a beeline for the area right under the water fountain, where it soaked up the remains of someone's drink. Ink from Lily's purple gel pen oozed sickeningly down the paper.

Reni turned from the classroom doorway, her brown eyes popping wide.

"Oh, no, you did not!" she said.

"Look at my homework!" Lily said. "I am so busted!"

Reni let her own backpack fall with a thud and dove for Lily's math binder that was splayed out near the trash can.

"No—get to class!" Lily said. "No point in both of us getting in trouble."

But the bell rang before Reni could answer, and a shadow fell over them from the doorway. It was Mrs. Reinhold.

"We're not late," Reni said to her, scrambling up with the last of Lily's belongings in both hands. "Lily dumped her backpack."

"I can see that," Mrs. Reinhold said.

She adjusted her almost-too-tiny-for-her-eyes glasses with the tips of both index fingers, as if she wanted to get a better focus on Lily, who was now using two arms to hug her backpack against her chest. Its contents poked out like yesterday's recycling pile.

Haven't you ever seen anybody spaz out before? Lily wanted to say to her. She was sure Mrs. Reinhold had. She'd probably been a seventh-grade English teacher since Noah was in middle school, and she'd definitely brought her disciplinary methods with her off the ark. Right now she was directing her pointed nose at Lily and frowning.

"If you had given yourself less time for visiting and more time for getting to class, Lilianna, this wouldn't have happened," Mrs. Reinhold said in the voice that always reminded Lily of cobwebs.

"Are you gonna mark us tardy?" Reni said.

" 'Gonna'?" Mrs. Reinhold said. "I'm not familiar with the word 'gonna.' "

Lily pulled her full lips into the biggest smile she could muster in the face of fear and slipped past Mrs. Reinhold toward her desk in the first row by the door. At least she didn't have to parade her trash heap of a backpack in front of the whole class. But Chelsea Gordon was sitting in Lily's seat and curling her lip at her as if Lily had yet again proven herself to be the biggest geek on the planet.

"Lilianna, you are now in the far row," Mrs. Reinhold's cobweb voice rang out behind her. "I've done some rearranging to eliminate the visiting that has been transpiring."

Lily's heart sank as her eyes moved in the direction the teacher was pointing. Ashley Adamson, Chelsea's best friend and closest clone, was sitting in front of Lily's new desk. No one could make Lily feel more like she'd just graduated from Un-cool School with high honors than Ashley.

"Do I have a new seat?" Reni asked.

"No," Mrs. Reinhold said. "I've separated you and Lilianna as well."

"But we don't talk!" Reni said.

"And I want to keep it that way."

Lily heard a few snickers as she crossed to her place by Ashley. At least Shad Shifferdecker's not in here, she told herself. He would already be standing on his chair, pointing out the purple gel ink that was now trailing down Lily's right leg. She slid into her seat, licked her fingers, and swiped at her leg.

"Please pass your homework forward," Mrs. Reinhold said. "And no, I will not answer any questions about it."

The Corn Chex Lily had eaten for breakfast turned to cement in her stomach as she looked at her homework paper. Only the parts around the edges were still legible. The rest looked like one of those inkblot tests they give mental patients.

She raised her hand.

"I said no questions," Mrs. Reinhold said.

"I just need to know if I can copy mine over really quick. It got water on it out in the hall—"

"Really 'quickly,'" Mrs. Reinhold said. "And no, you may not."

Why was it that the woman answered every question with a grammar lesson? Lily was dying to know if Reni had noticed that, but there was no asking her, as far away as she was now sitting. Lily scanned the room again and found Suzy, her other closest friend. Mrs. Reinhold hadn't moved her either. Why would she? Suzy never did anything wrong.

"So are you gonna pass in your paper or what?"

Lily jerked her head around. Ashley was looking at her, lip in its usual curl. The only time it wasn't rolled up under her nose was when she was flirting with some boy.

"Here," Lily said. She thrust her soggy paper forward.

Ashley's lip nearly went up into her nostrils. "Gross! What did you do, use it for a towel?"

"Ashley, am I to assume that if I put you back there next to the pencil sharpener you would strike up a conversation with it as well?"

Mrs. Reinhold was pointing her nose at Ashley, who snatched the paper out of Lily's hand and stuck the whole row's pile out at Mrs. R. As soon as Mrs. Reinhold's back was turned, Ashley whirled around and frosted Lily with an icy stare.

Like it was MY fault! Lily thought. But she didn't say a word. She didn't even glance over at Reni or Suzy to read what their faces were saying. She'd had enough direct contact with Mrs. Reinhold for one day.

But evidently not in Mrs. Reinhold's opinion. As soon as she'd given the reading assignment and Lily had her head buried in her book, Mrs. Reinhold said, "Lilianna, I need to speak with you."

Lily could feel her usually pale face going blotchy the way it always did when she felt doom breathing down her neck. Slowly, she untangled her long legs from the desk and made her way up front. Mrs. Reinhold pulled the chair next to her desk in closer and motioned for Lily to sit down.

"I'm sorry about my homework," Lily whispered. "When I dropped everything, it ended up under the water fountain and—"

"I'm not concerned about your homework assignment at the moment, Lilianna," she said. "I want to speak to you about—"

"I won't talk to Ashley—I really won't—"

"How can I count on that?" Mrs. Reinhold said. "You won't even stop talking to me long enough for me to get a word in. Now, are you finished?"

Lily nodded.

"I have been looking over the writing that you have turned in so far, and I have noticed that you are competent in composition."

Lily blinked. "Is that bad?"

"No. 'Competent' means that your writing is adequate." She shook her head. "What are they teaching in elementary school these days?"

"Do you want me to answer that?" Lily said.

"No. I want you to take this to Room D–208 during lunch today and give it to Mr. Miniver. It's a note recommending you for the newspaper staff."

"Me?" Lily said. "I've never worked on a newspaper before."

"Of course you haven't. You're twelve years old. That is precisely what school is for—to expose you to experiences you have not yet had."

"What will I be doing?" Lily said. "I mean—do I get to be a reporter and interview people?"

The image of herself dashing around with a notebook in one hand and a mini-tape recorder in the other was already vivid in Lily's head, and words like "scoop" and "fast-breaking" were shouting in her ears.

"I'm sure Mr. Miniver will tell you everything you need to know." Mrs. Reinhold adjusted her glasses with her fingertips again. "That is, if you will give him an opportunity to speak, Lilianna."

"I will!" Lily said. "And, um, Mrs. Reinhold, could you please call me Lily?"

"Is that your proper name?"

"Well, it's short for Lilianna, which I guess you could say is my proper name."

"Then I'll continue to call you Lilianna."

And I'll continue to call you Mrs. Noah, Lily thought as she tucked herself back into her desk, but she'd never say it out loud, of course. Just thinking she was going to be busted by the woman had been enough to give Lily cardiac arrest. This was one lady she was not going to cross again.

Once that was settled in her mind, thoughts of being the new star reporter for the *Middle School Mirror* took over. She could barely concentrate on her reading assignment between planning a whole new wardrobe so she could look like the women on the news and glancing at the clock to see how much longer it would be before they'd be out of class so she could tell Reni and Suzy. And then she'd have to find Kresha and Zooey and tell them.

After an eternity, the bell rang, and it was all Lily could do not to knock Ashley over getting to the door. As it was, Ashley gave her a sneer and said, "Chill out, Robbins."

"What did Mrs. Reinhold say to you?" Reni said when they were outside.

"Did you get in trouble?" Suzy asked. Her delicate dark eyebrows came together as if she were awaiting Lily's death sentence.

Lily's grin went earlobe to earlobe as she told them. And it went even farther when they caught up with Kresha and Zooey at the lockers, and she gave them the good news too.

Zooey, who was red-faced from rushing up the stairs after gym class, couldn't get her breath enough to say anything. Kresha said plenty—but most of it Lily couldn't understand. Kresha was Croatian, and between the accent and the Croatian words she threw in when English failed her, it was sometimes tough to have a conversation. Still, all the Girlz (as they called each other) were excited for her—for about two minutes anyway.

Then Zooey said, "They're going to kill me in PE. We did aerobics the whole period again!"

"You'll live," Reni said.

"Lee-lee, I have news too!" Kresha said.

"Slowly, Kresha," Suzy said. "Tell it slowly." She was Kresha's best coach.

"You know I take Een-glish class in summer," Kresha said.

The Girlz all nodded, including Lily, although she wasn't sure what this had to do with her being a reporter.

"I doing so well, my ESL teacher say I being pro- … pro-"

"Promoted?" Suzy said.

"Ya! Promoted to next the level."

"What's ESL again?" Zooey asked.

"English as a second language," Suzy told her.

"Soon it be my first language!" Kresha said. She was so excited her straggly light-brown bangs were dancing across her forehead.

"We need to get to geography," Suzy said. She was looking nervously at her watch.

"We'll all talk at lunch," Reni said. "Meet at our regular table."

"I can't," Lily said. "Remember? I have to go see the newspaper guy."

Four faces looked back at her with identically raised eyebrows.

"You're gonna have to miss Girlz Club to do this reporter thing?" Zooey asked.

"You can't," Reni said. "It's our only time to all be together."

"Maybe it'll just be today—"

"It better be," Kresha said.

"Gee, Kresha," Zooey said. "That sounded like real English!"

"Come on—we're gonna be late!" Suzy said.

They scattered to their classes—Suzy, Reni, and Lily scurrying for geography, and Zooey and Kresha heading for reading. Lily's thoughts were going in at least that many directions.

Nobody's as jazzed as I am about the newspaper, she thought. *Don't they know how long I've waited to find my thing?*

They should by now, she decided, as she sank into her desk in geography class. She'd been trying since sixth grade to figure out what would make her special. Everybody in her family stood out in some way. Dad was a professor who knew everything in life about C. S. Lewis and about medieval literature. Mom was a phys ed teacher at the high school who always had a winning girls' volleyball team. Lily's older brother Art was Mr. Band at the high school, and even her younger brother Joe was Junior Jock. Only Lily hadn't found her niche.

She'd tried a bunch of stuff—modeling, first aid, women's lib, entertaining like Martha Stewart—and the Girlz had been through it all with her. Even though she'd been pretty good at all of those and had learned other stuff—life stuff—none of them had turned out to be what could make her who she was meant to be.

But this newspaper thing, she thought, *could be the ticket!*

She sneaked a look at the clock while Ms. Ferringer was looking for a missing map transparency for the overhead. Would lunchtime never come?

"Has anybody seen my map of Africa?" Ms. Ferringer asked.

It was her first year of teaching, and as far as Lily could tell, it wasn't going all that well. If she wasn't looking for a map, she was searching for her pencil, which was usually on top of her head halfway holding her blonde hair into some bun concoction.

"Somebody in my last class probably took it," Ms. Ferringer mumbled as she pawed through a folder on her desk.

"Is Shad Shifferdecker in that class?" Lily asked.

Ms. Ferringer nodded absently.

"Then there's your trouble," Lily said.

The class snickered in unison.

"You got that right," Ms. Ferringer said, grinning too. Then she put her hand up to her mouth and blinked her big green eyes about eighty times. "That was so unprofessional. Forget I said that," she said. "That doesn't leave this room."

Don't count on it, Lily thought. Even now, Ashley was whispering furiously to Chelsea, and Marcie McCleary was almost falling out of her seat trying to get in on the conversation. Rumor had it that Ashley and Shad were "going out," although where anybody in seventh grade went when they "went out" was always beyond Lily. Besides, who would want to go anywhere with Shad Shifferdecker?

When lunchtime finally did crawl around, Lily was in Room D–208 almost before the fourth-period students could get out of it. Her head filled to capacity with ideas for news stories, her hand already on the sharpened pencil in the pocket of her cargo pants, Lily walked up to the small, slim man with the mustache behind the desk and stuck out her hand.

"Hi," she said in her most professional voice. "I'm Lily Robbins. I'm your new reporter."

The mustache twitched, and the blue eyes that swam under contact lenses twinkled at her.

"Oh, you are, are you?" he said.

"Yes," Lily said. "I have references. Well, one reference—from Mrs. Reinhold." She handed him the note. "I am in the right place, aren't I? This is the newspaper staff room, right?"

"This is the staff room, and it looks like you're on the staff. Welcome, Lily."

Lily looked around with a possessive eye. There were several computers lined up under the window, and there was a big table in the middle of the room with a special light hanging over it. She could practically see herself bent over it, pencil behind her ear, conferring in serious tones with the rest of the staff over a piece about—what? A bomb threat? A teachers' strike?

"But I hope you're not too disappointed," Mr. Miniver said.

Lily came back to the present and blinked at him.

"You can definitely be on the newspaper staff," he said. "But, Lily—" He gave her a kind smile. "You can't be a reporter."

All Lily could think of to say was, "Oh."

"You are disappointed," Mr. Miniver said.

"No!" Lily lied. "Um—so what am I going to be doing?"

"That's the spirit!" Mr. Miniver darted out from behind the desk like a startled squirrel. Even his mustache seemed to come to life. "There are a lot of jobs for newcomers," he said. "You can sell ads, do copyediting—Mrs. Reinhold says your spelling is excellent—" The mustache twitched. "I don't imagine she hands out that compliment very often."

It didn't do anything for Lily. The thought of sitting around correcting other people's spelling was right up there with emptying the dishwasher.

"I was hoping I'd get to write," Lily said.

The mustache drooped. Lily was figuring out that you could pretty much tell what Mr. Miniver's emotions were at any given moment if you just watched his upper lip.

"We have plenty of writers," he said, "and they're all eighth graders. I'm sure you've noticed that seventh graders have a hard time breaking into anything around here. I think they call it paying your dues. I'm sorry."

He really did look sorry, and that made Lily brave enough to say, "So how do I pay my dues?"

"I like you!" The mustache turned upward. "Okay—here's what you do—you come in here every day at lunch and do whatever little odds and ends we have for you to do and sit in on some of our meetings. Who knows, maybe some story will come up that nobody wants to do, and the editor will let you do it."

"Who's the editor?" Lily asked.

"That would be Lance Adamson."

"Is that Ashley Adamson's brother?" Lily said.

"I think Lance does have a sister, yes. The little blonde?"

"Yeah," Lily said reluctantly.

"I let Lance make as many editorial decisions as I can," Mr. Miniver said. "If you prove yourself to him, who knows, you might be the first seventh grader to become a reporter."

His eyes looked as if they were about to twinkle right out of their sockets, but Lily couldn't get excited. Once Ashley found out Lily was working with her brother, she'd give him an earful about what a geek she thought Lily was, and Lily could count on correcting spelling until she was a senior in high school.

"Now—I do have one other idea," Mr. Miniver said, stroking his mustache with slim fingers. "We're in need of some fun columns for filler, and so far nobody's come up with any ideas that do it for us."

"Columns?" Lily said.

"Regular little articles that aren't news—they just have information. In the *Burlington County Times*, for instance, they have a daily column on ways to save time—then there's a little health feature—"

"Oh," Lily said. That didn't sound too thrilling.

"I tell you what," Mr. Miniver said, "since you seem so determined, why don't you look at the *Times* and see if you can figure out what I'm talking about. Then if you come up with any ideas, we'll hear them at the meeting tomorrow."

"Okay," Lily said.

Then, because he was looking at her with such hope in his mustache, she said, "I'm sure I'll come up with something."

"You know what?" he said. "I'm sure you will!"

Later, when Lily met her best friend at their lockers, Reni asked, "How was Mr. Miniver?" She was squatting at her locker just below Lily's.

"He reminds me of an exclamation point with a mustache," Lily said.

"So what's your first story? Hey, maybe you could do one on the orchestra!"

Lily looked down at the dusty-brown cornrows on top of Reni's head. She was glad Reni wasn't looking up at her, or she'd have seen the "no thanks" in Lily's eyes. *Nobody's gonna want to read about the orchestra,* she thought.

But what would kids want to read about? Lily was pondering that in fifth-period pre-algebra when she felt a tap on her shoulder. She turned around with a sigh to face Marcie McCleary. Too bad Mr. Chester, their math teacher, didn't mind them talking in his class or she could have used that as an excuse not to have to answer Marcie. Lily would have bet her whole supply of gel pens that Marcie was going to ask something nosy.

"Do you have any Kleenex?" Marcie said.

"Yeah," Lily said impatiently, and she was about to go for her backpack when she realized Marcie was crying. She definitely needed several Kleenex. Even her nose was running.

"What's wrong?" Lily said, piling three tissues onto Marcie's desk.

"Everything in this whole stupid school!"

"Oh," Lily said.

She started to turn back around, but Marcie let out an especially loud sob, and with it came the rest of "everything."

"Today—I'm trying to talk to Ashley and Chelsea between classes—and then it gets late—and then I have to run to class—and then I get written up for running in the halls—and then the next period I'm trying to find Ashley, and I'm looking back over my shoulder, and I accidentally go up the down staircase, and this eighth grader calls me a moron, so I go in the bathroom so I can cry in private, and I get written up for being in there without a pass!" Marcie stopped to take a breath.

I thought I had it bad! Lily thought. She'd never especially liked Marcie because she was always trying to elbow her way into the in crowd with Ashley and Chelsea and their friends, and often doing her own version of the curled lip at Lily and the Girlz in the process. Still, right now, Lily felt sorry for her. If anybody knew what it was like to get the middle-school blues, it was Lily.

"Every time I turn around, I do something else wrong," Marcie said.

"So don't turn around."

Marcie glared at Lily through her tears. "Gee, thanks."

"No, I'm serious. I think I know what your problem is."

"What?"

"You really want to know?"

Marcie sniffed and nodded.

"Every time you got in trouble today it was because of Ashley and Chelsea," Lily said.

"Nuh-uh!"

"You're talking to Ashley, and you're late. You're looking for Ashley, and you go up the wrong stairs. And where's Ashley when you get busted?"

"I don't know."

"Right. I hope this doesn't hurt your feelings, but I don't think Ashley and Chelsea care about you half as much as you do about them. So why mess everything up because of them?"

"Because I won't have anybody else to hang out with!" Marcie wailed.

"What are you talking about?" Lily said. She swept an arm at the room where twenty-five other heads were in various stages of pre-algebra homework. "There are all kinds of people to hang out with!"

"No—"

"You just haven't tried, Marcie," Lily said. "You've been too busy chasing after Ashley like you're a little puppy and she's got the Puppy Chow!"

Marcie's next sob turned into a snort.

"I mean it!" Lily said. "They say 'heel' and you do—and then they say 'sit' and you do—and then they run off and leave you there."

Marcie's snorts were now juicy giggles, and her face was ketchup red. "Stop, Lily!" she said. "You're making me laugh!"

"Who needs them? Get your own friends—people who really like you."

"You think I could?" Marcie asked.

"Why not? Do you have leprosy or something?"

Marcie started to giggle so hard she had to ask Mr. Chester for the restroom pass so she could get control. Mr. Chester, who had a gray crew cut and pictures of his grandkids on his desk, said to Lily, "There's nothing sillier than a twelve-year-old girl. She'll be crying in a minute."

"Nah, she already did that," Lily said.

Mr. Chester chuckled. "You've got quite a sense of humor, Lily."

She lost her humor though when she got home and couldn't find that day's copy of the *Burlington County Times*.

Dad was the only one home, and it was ridiculous to ask him. Dad could never find his glasses, his briefcase, his pen, or his dog-eared copy of *The Lion, the Witch, and the Wardrobe*—much less the *Burlington County Times*.

Lily finally located the newspaper in the laundry basket and sank into one of the recliners to study it. She frowned her way through the first section with no success.

There were columns, all right, just like Mr. Miniver had said. But "Harriet's Household Hints" and somebody or other's political insights didn't give her any ideas. As far as Lily was concerned, the whole paper was pretty boring. She was into section D before she saw anything that even caught her eye. It was actually some letters, written back and forth.

"Dear Abby," they all started. "My husband and I have been married for thirty-five years and he—"

Lily read on about husbands who wouldn't pull a weed and kids who were smoking it. Abby, whoever she was, had an answer for everybody, and most of the time the way she put things made Lily laugh out loud.

"Entertaining yourself, Lil?" Mom said as she passed the family room on her way in from volleyball practice.

"Hey, Mom," Lily said, "do you ever read this 'Dear Abby' person's column?"

"Every day for years," Mom said. "I get a kick out of her." Her mouth did the twitchy thing it did instead of smiling.

Lily sighed. She had come up with only one possible idea, but she wasn't going to present it. The staff would probably love an advice column, but they sure weren't going to let Lily write it.

Who's gonna pay any attention to anything I have to say?

"Set the table, would you, Lil?" Mom called from the kitchen.

"It's Art's turn!" Lily said.

"And put on steak knives. The meat could be a little tough."

Certainly nobody in THIS family ever listens to me!

That night after supper, Lily was proven right—no one listened to a word she said, so she went up in her room. Petting Otto, her beloved mutt, with one hand, Lily worked on her math homework with the other.

"If I hadn't been counseling Marcie during class, I could've gotten this done," she said to Otto.

He cocked his wiry-haired, gray head at her pencil.

"No," she said. "No!"

Too late! He pounced, snatching her last pencil with a good eraser in his jaws, and retreated under the bed with it. She was hanging down, hair mopping the floor, when her door opened.

"That thing about blood going to your brain making you think better is a myth," her brother Art said. "Give it up."

"Don't you ever knock?" Lily asked.

She pulled her head up. Under the bed, Otto growled.

"Don't worry about it," Art said. "I'm not staying. I know when I'm not welcome. Oh—the phone's for you."

He handed Lily the portable phone and slipped out, eyes fastened warily on Otto. Art was the one who had brought Otto home from the pound last summer, but Lily was the only one Otto tolerated.

"Hello?" she said into the phone.

There was silence and then a dial tone.

"Hello?" Lily said again.

The phone kept toning away, until Lily pushed the off button and took it up the steps to Art's attic room.

"Who was it?" she said as she burst through his door.

"Don't you ever knock?" he said.

"Who was on the phone?"

"One of your little girlfriends. I didn't ask." He smirked as he ran a hand over his very curly but short red hair. "Why? Can't you tell them apart either?"

"Yeah, but there was nobody there when I said hello."

"Maybe she changed her mind."

"What did she sound like?"

"I don't know!" Art said. "They all sound the same."

"No, they don't!"

"I take it back," Art said. "This one wasn't giggling. They usually giggle when I answer the phone."

That was because they all thought he was "cute," but Lily sure wasn't going to tell him that.

Lily went back to doing homework and then read in her Bible and wrote in her journal, the whole time wishing she could come up with a column idea.

"But I can't just wish," she wrote. "I have to pray. God, could you help me out here? I'm kind of stuck."

Lily fell asleep, hugging Otto and her big stuffed panda, China, and dreamed about "Dear Abby" writing her a letter. It was all in purple gel ink that got wet and ran all over the bed. She woke up to a puddle of Otto's drool.

The next morning at school, Lily hurried to get to her locker and then to the bench by the stairs where she and the Girlz always met before classes. If she was going to be in the newspaper room every day at lunch, this might be the only time she'd see them all.

She'd just sat down and was rechecking the zipper on her backpack when somebody came running toward her. She suddenly had an armful of Marcie McCleary.

"Lily, I love you!" she said as she flung her arms around Lily's neck.

"Me?" Lily said. "Why?" She looked around over Marcie's shoulder to make sure nobody was watching.

"Because you were right!" Marcie pulled away, and Lily saw that her freckled face was glowing as if she'd just been crowned Miss America.

"About what?" Lily said.

"About the friend thing! I didn't call Ashley or Chelsea or any of them last night. I got out the school directory. You know, the one we got at orientation? And I just started reading names until I found Heidi—you know, Hinson—and I called her. She was, like, so happy to hear from me because she's been getting in so much trouble and her parents won't let her hang out with any of her friends anymore. Anyway, we're gonna meet at lunch, and we're already planning to go to the movies Saturday if her mom will let her out of the house, which she probably will because it's with me. I never get in any trouble, except those last two times, but her mom doesn't know about that and that's nothing compared to what Heidi's old friends did— "

Marcie took a breath and seemed ready to start in again. Lily said quickly, "That's cool, Marcie."

"It's because of you," Marcie said. "You gave me, like, the best advice. My mom even said so." She looked furtively over her shoulder and whispered, "She never liked Ashley and them that much."

"Don't you hate it when moms are right?" Lily said.

Marcie gave a huge guffaw. Lily just waited. Any minute now she expected Marcie to get hysterical and have to run for the bathroom. But Marcie took off at a fast walk, telling Lily there'd be no more write-ups for her.

Lily thought about what Marcie had just told her: *You gave me, like, the best advice*. Lily patted her pocket and found her pencil. Ripping a piece of paper out of the first binder she came to in her backpack, she settled down on the bench and started to write.

"Didn't you finish your homework, Lily?" she heard Suzy say in a worried voice a few minutes later.

"Yeah," Lily said. "I'm writing up this idea to present to the newspaper staff. Listen to this and tell me what you think."

Suzy nodded and sat next to her on the bench. Lily cleared her throat.

Dear Advice Person:

I have these two girls that I want to be friends with, only they don't like me as much as I like them. I always have to be the one to call or find them, and it seems like every time I turn around, I'm getting in trouble because of it. What do I do?

—Middle-School Blues

Dear Blues:

That's simple. Just don't turn around.

—Lily

Chapter 3

Suzy loved the idea. So did Zooey. Lily wasn't sure about Kresha. She nodded about a million times, but you could never be certain whether she'd really understood everything you said.

"So, are you going to present that to the staff?" Suzy said. "In front of all those eighth graders?"

"You're so brave," Zooey said, hazel eyes wide.

"I think so," Lily said. But there was still one more person she wanted to run it by, and Reni didn't show up at the bench. When the five-minute warning bell rang, she was still nowhere in sight.

Reni wasn't in either of Lily's first two classes, and by the time she got to English in third period, Lily was about to explode. She hung around at the door, craning her neck above the mass of middle schoolers thronging past her, but she still hadn't caught sight of Reni when Mrs. Reinhold's cobwebs spun behind her.

"Are you planning to make tardiness a habit, Lilianna?" she said. "If you are, I'll have to make calling your parents a habit."

"No!" Lily said—and with one last glance down the hall, she dove into the classroom and scurried to her desk.

Chelsea was sitting in it. She and Ashley looked up at her, and for a second Lily thought she was seeing double. They were looking more alike all the time. They both had their shortish hair in crooked parts. They were wearing almost identical white Gap tops. And the curl of their lips could have come from the same DNA.

"You're in my seat," Lily said to Chelsea.

"Am I really?" Chelsea said. "Duh!" She looked at Ashley, and they rolled their eyes in unison.

Lily glanced nervously at the clock. "The bell's gonna ring."

"How about telling us something we don't already know," Ashley said.

"Yeah," Chelsea said, "like why your hair does that."

"Does what?" Lily said. She put a hand up to her mass of red hair, but it felt like it was doing what it always did—sticking out in all directions like a lion's mane.

Chelsea glanced at Ashley, who glanced back, and Lily knew they were having a conversation that didn't require words. She and Reni had those all the time.

Evidently, Chelsea got the go-ahead from Ashley because she said, "I don't know what it's doing. That's just it."

"I count not being in your correct seat as a tardy," Mrs. Reinhold said.

Ashley and Chelsea both rolled their eyes this time, and Ashley murmured, "She is such a witch."

"No doubt," Chelsea said.

She began to withdraw her petite self out of the desk so slowly it was all Lily could do not to help her—by snatching her out by the hair. When Chelsea finally vacated Lily's seat, she didn't head for her own desk. Instead, she put her glossy lips next to Lily's ear and whispered, "You look like Ronald McDonald."

All Lily could do was stare as Chelsea did a fast walk past Mrs. Reinhold, smiling at the two guys in the front row as if to say, "Have you noticed how adorable I am?"

Chelsea slid into her desk just as the bell rang. Reni had evidently managed to get to hers while Lily was having the bad hair day conversation with Chelsea and Ashley. Only when Mrs. Reinhold pointed her nose at Lily did she realize that she herself was still standing up. Face going blotchy-hot, Lily made a lunge for her seat. Her left fanny cheek hit the back of the chair as she tumbled in, still wearing her backpack. She was so squished up against the desktop she could barely breathe.

What's the point in breathing anyway? she thought. *I'm gonna die any second.*

Mrs. Reinhold gave a sniff up her pointy nose, adjusted her teeny-weeny glasses with her index fingers, and made a notation in her grade book. Lily could almost hear her mom saying, "Lil, I'm disappointed. We've never gotten a call from school about any of you kids before."

Somehow, that wasn't the uniqueness Lily had in mind. What she did have in mind was the advice column, and she really wanted Reni's opinion. But right now Reni was digging through her backpack as was everybody else in the room.

"Am I gonna have to ask you for your paper every day?" Ashley said, her hand with its blue-glittered nails extended. "Who am I, your mother?"

You are SO not my mother! Lily thought. But she bit her lip and with a wary eye on Mrs. Reinhold pulled out her homework.

"What?" Ashley said as she took it and stared at it. "You didn't wash your face with it today?"

"Ladies." It was the cobweb voice.

"Yes?" Lily said. She knew three more blotches were appearing on her neck.

"This is your final warning," Mrs. Reinhold said. "Once class has started, there will be no talking unless I give permission. I'm certain I've made myself clear on that."

She looked as if she expected an answer, so Lily nodded. Ashley did nothing.

How come I'm the one taking the flack? Lily thought. *It's Ashley who's doing it all!*

Mrs. Reinhold went on to give the day's assignment—an essay about "The Lottery." Then she sat down to grade last night's homework while pens began scratching across sheets of paper.

"Like I care about 'The Lottery,'" Lily heard Ashley mutter.

Lily was pretty sure nobody else cared either, except about the grade. But she bent her head over her binder and wrote with everything she had. It was hard to ignore the shadow of her hair on the paper, and a few times she did stop to wonder whether it really did make her look like Ronald McDonald, but mostly she concentrated on creating an essay that would pop Mrs. Reinhold's glasses right off of her pointy nose.

She was so focused that she finished before anybody else did. Immediately, her mind flipped back to the column and to Reni.

Reni was chewing on her eraser, and from the way her bunchy lips were set, Lily knew she was either way into her essay or working out some other biggie in her head. In either case, she obviously didn't realize Lily wanted to tell her something with her eyes.

Look at me, Lily thought as hard as she could. But Reni didn't.

With a cautious glance at Mrs. Reinhold to make sure she was absorbed in the grammatical disasters on last night's homework, Lily silently pulled another piece of paper out of her binder and took the cap off her purple gel pen.

TO: Reni
FROM: Lily

Where were you this a.m.? Meet me after class. Have something to show you. Need your opinion.

It was all she dared write down. Mrs. Reinhold, she was certain, had some kind of radar that automatically alerted her when somebody was breaking one of her 810,000 rules. She had never said anything about passing notes, but Lily didn't think you had to be a brain surgeon to figure out that it was probably grounds for execution or something. Still, there had to be a way.

In front of her, Lily heard a muffled snicker, and she looked up to see Ashley trading looks with Chelsea across the room. Mrs. Reinhold looked up, but by then Ashley had her head conscientiously buried in *Adventures in World Literature.* It was Lily's eyes she caught.

"Are you finished, Lilianna?" she said.

Lily nodded.

"Let me have your paper, then. Go get a grammar book and start your homework."

In one big sweep, she pointed to the assignment on the board and then to the row of grammar texts on the shelf on the other side of the room—the very side Reni sat on.

Lily smothered a smile with one hand as she tucked the folded note into the other and strolled casually to the bookshelf. Picking up an English Usage Book I, she sneaked a look at Mrs. Reinhold, who was going after some poor kid's paper with her red pen like she was stabbing ants. Lily dropped the note into Reni's lap and hurried back to her seat. She knew her entire face was one big mass of blotches.

I'd never make it as a spy, she thought. She didn't even dare look to see if Reni was unfolding it. She just whipped open her grammar book and pretended correct comma usage was her life's desire.

When the bell rang, Mrs. Reinhold chose that day to start dismissing them by rows, and Lily's was the last one.

"Someone has to teach you not to behave like a herd of cattle," she said.

Wishing for a cattle prod, Lily finally got out the door to find Reni standing first on one foot and then the other, lips bunched up impatiently.

"Hurry up!" she said. "I have to get Ms. Ferringer to sign my permission slip before class starts."

She took off down the hall with Lily trotting after her.

"What permission slip?" Lily asked.

"To go to the orchestra room after I finish my work in geography. Mr. Lamb's got me learning a special piece, and this is his free period, so he can help me." She looked at Lily with sparkling eyes. "I'm so glad I took private lessons this summer. I bet I get to go to State—"

Lily wanted to blurt out, "What about my note?" But instead she said, "Cool. Really—that's so cool."

"So hurry up and tell me what you wanted to show me," Reni said.

She dodged around an eighth-grade couple, who were walking as slowly as possible so they could stare into each other's eyes, and Lily had to scramble to catch up.

When she did, Reni said, "Why'd you write the note so weird? It was like a telegram or something." She grinned. "A Lily-Gram!"

"I didn't want Mrs. Reinhold catching me. I think she hates me."

"Yesterday you thought she liked you."

"Forget that!" Lily said. She reached into her backpack and took out the advice column. "Read this and tell me what you think."

"If I have time," Reni said.

"Well—yikes," Lily said. There was a day when Reni had always had time when it came to the other Girlz—especially Lily. She could feel her face sagging.

"Okay—I'll do it," Reni said. "While Ms. Ferringer is looking for her pencil."

Lily gave a relieved laugh. "Then write me—tell me what you think of it as an idea for the paper."

"It's gonna have to be a Lily-Gram," Reni said.

"Lily-Gram?" said a voice ahead of them. "More like a Lame-Gram."

Lily had to grab on to Reni's arm to keep from moaning out loud. It was Shad Shifferdecker, sauntering out of Ms. Ferringer's room with his jeans, as usual, hanging down around what there was of his skinny hips. Lily had barely seen him in the few weeks since school had started, and that was one of the things she DID like about middle school. She hadn't had to look at his sneering mouth full of braces or listen to his evil comments. Until now.

"Whatever you want to call it," Reni said to him. "It doesn't matter, 'cause it's none of your business."

"Like I care anyway," he said. But the way he slid his narrowed eyes over Lily, she knew he was doing what he always did—looking for a way to get to her. For a little while last spring, they had actually been civil to each other. But when he tried to wreck Lily's party over the summer, that had taken them right back to not being able to stand the sight of each other. For somebody who couldn't bear to look at her, he sure took inventory whenever he got the chance.

"What are you looking at, Shad?" Reni said.

His mouth twisted into one of his famous sneers as he looked right at Lily. "Nothin'," he said.

"Why did you even ask him that?" Lily said as he meandered off down the hall like he was strolling through the mall.

Reni didn't have a chance to answer. Ashley burst out of the classroom, right into their path, and practically mowed both of them down to get out to the middle of the hall.

"Sha-ad!" she shouted. "Come back here!"

"No, don't, Shad," Lily said to Reni as they managed to get into the room. "Nobody wants you here."

"She does," Reni said. "But I sure don't know why."

"Forget them," Lily said. "Read my thing."

Ms. Ferringer did take the predicted five minutes to find everything she needed. It was just long enough for Reni to scan Lily's proposal and get busy on a Lily-Gram. Before she left for the orchestra room, face beaming, she dropped a folded-up piece of paper on Lily's map of the Middle East. Lily stopped her current thought—which was why all the names of Middle Eastern cities sounded like Dr. Seuss had made them up—and hungrily opened the note.

Lily-Gram

TO: Lily
FROM: Reni

Cool idea. Praying for you. Pray for me too.

Lily refolded the paper feeling a little disappointed. She'd hoped for a little more enthusiasm from Reni.

Of course, it IS a Lily-Gram, she thought. *It's gotta be short or it doesn't work.*

She grabbed a piece of paper and made the Lily-Gram logo at the top. It was clear they were going to have to copy a bunch of these to save having to redo the heading every time.

She wrote: "Thanks. Praying."

She was about to go back to trying to find the Gaza Strip on the map when another thought struck her. If she said she was going to pray for Reni, she probably ought to do it now before she forgot.

Thanks for Reni, God, she prayed to herself with eyes half-closed above the map. *And please be with her. Amen.*

She knew it was short, but she had to get this stupid map done. *Maybe I oughta call it a God-Gram,* she thought.

When the bell rang, Lily bolted for the door, proposal in hand.

"Aren't you going to lunch?" Suzy said behind her.

"Gotta go to the newspaper room, remember?" Lily said.

"Oh," Suzy said. Her almost-not-there dark eyebrows came together in a sad frown. "I thought maybe we could talk."

"Write me a Lily-Gram," Lily said. By now she was backing down the hall, drawing jeers from several eighth graders she plowed into.

"A what?" Suzy said.

But she was suddenly swallowed up in the crowd. *I can tell her later,* Lily thought, and she made tracks to D–208.

The room was still empty when she got there except for one boy who was sitting on Mr. Miniver's desk, swinging his legs. He had a square jaw and blue eyes that sizzled even from across the classroom. What caught Lily's attention was his hair. It was short and spiky and so perfectly gelled he looked like he could have been one of those male models in *Seventeen* magazine—the kind she'd heard Ashley and Chelsea call "babes." If Art even attempted to look that perfect, Lily knew she'd have laughed herself silly. But this guy obviously was not somebody you laughed at.

"Uh, this is the newspaper room," the boy said. "We're about to have a meeting. Staff only."

"I'm staff," Lily said.

"Since when?"

"Since yesterday."

"Nobody told me."

Lily shifted her backpack uneasily. "Maybe they didn't think you'd care."

The boy let air out through his lips. "Du-uh," he said. "I'm only the editor."

"Oh," was all Lily could say, although about a thousand thoughts were tripping over each other in her head. This was Lance Adamson. All the Adamsons must have been born rude. He was in charge of this paper. And she'd just made the lamest impression possible.

"So who are you?" he said.

"Um, Mr. Miniver said I could be on staff."

"Yes, I did!" a voice sang out behind her. "Lily—welcome back! I see you've met Lancelot."

Mr. Miniver's mustache was practically doing the tango, and he bounced around Lily to his desk like he was attached to an exclamation point that never stopped moving.

"He's the only one who calls me that," Lance said to Lily. "So don't try it."

"Oh, I won't!" Lily said. "I get annoyed when anybody but my dad calls me Lilliputian."

Lance's face scrunched. "What?"

But he didn't wait for an explanation. The rest of the newspaper staff came through the door in one big mass just then, and they all dragged chairs into a semicircle around Lance. Lily tried to do the same, but by the time she got free of her backpack and found an extra chair, there were no slots left in the semicircle, and she had to park behind a too-big-to-be-in-eighth-grade boy who blocked her view of Lance and Mr. Miniver and just about anything else beyond him with his shoulders.

"Call the meeting to order, Lancelot" Mr. Miniver sang out. "Let's get started."

"Yeah, let's get started," Lance said. "Who's got the front page stuff?"

Three hands went up. Lily wished hers had been among them, but at that point, it didn't seem like she'd ever be raising her hand about anything in this room. She curled her fingers around her proposal and tried not to look too pathetic.

"What about you, Crystal?" Mr. Miniver said. "Don't you have a front-page piece?"

"Yeah," Lance said. "You were supposed to write one up on that bus driver. The one that took the whole busload to the police station when that one kid wouldn't stop yellin' stuff out the windows."

Lily couldn't see the Crystal in question because of Shoulders, but she could imagine the face that went with the wilted voice that said, "I didn't get it."

"Dude, you said you would!" Lance said.

Lily pictured his blue eyes burning a hole into Crystal. She heard Mr. Miniver clear his throat.

"I'm sure Crystal has a good reason—"

"I do!" said the frail little voice. "I tried to talk to that bus driver, but he was so—like, mean—"

"Well, duh!" said Shoulders. "That's the whole point of the story. The dude's a jerk!"

"That isn't good journalism, Doug!" Mr. Miniver said. Lily stretched her neck to see him. Although his mustache was on alert, his voice was still coming up into exclamation points at the ends of his sentences.

"So who's gonna do the story?" Lance said.

"Not me," said one girl. Several others nodded.

"How 'bout you, Dougie?" Crystal said.

"Nah," Shoulders said. "I already got enough to do."

There was an uneasy silence while everybody Lily could see stared down at their laps. Mr. Miniver stroked his mustache with his thin fingers, but he didn't say anything.

Here's your chance, Lily, her thoughts told her.

Face already turning into a red and white map of the Gaza Strip, Lily slowly raised her hand. When nobody saw it, she got up on one knee and waved it over Doug's head.

"Looks like you have a volunteer," Mr. Miniver said.

Lance looked at Lily as if he'd never seen her before. Naturally, his lip curled.

"Aren't you a seventh grader?" he said.

"Yes," Lily said. "But if nobody else wants to do it—"

Another hand shot up—a girl with hair down to her waist, which she tossed impatiently over her shoulder.

"KJ?" Mr. Miniver said to her.

"It's a rule," she said. "No seventh grader can be a reporter."

Mr. Miniver's mustache smiled. "Does that mean you're offering to do the story? If not, I don't see that Lance has any other choice but to give it to Lily."

Lance looked as if he didn't much care for not having any other choice. At that moment, except for the hair, Lily thought he was the spitting, curled-lip image of Ashley.

"Never mind," he said. "I'll do it myself."

Lily sagged. But Mr. Miniver's mustache didn't even quiver from its smile. "But I still think Lily's enthusiasm needs to be put to good use," he said. "Since no one else on the staff has offered any column ideas, I've asked her to come up with some."

Everybody either squirmed or looked at the ceiling. No one even darted an eye in Lily's direction.

"If we don't get some seventh graders involved, there won't be a newspaper next year," Mr. Miniver said. "You were all given a chance last year ..."

"Yeah, sure," Lance said. He folded his arms across his chest. "Columns are grunt work anyway."

Grunt work? Lily thought. She felt like grunting, right at him.

But they were all looking at her now, every face giving some version of "Oh, this oughta be good." Lily had the urge to tear up the proposal and give it to them as confetti. If Lance hadn't done the lip thing just then, she might have. But the anger prickled up her backbone, and she unfolded her proposal with a snap.

"Here's my idea," she said. And she gave it to them, complete with the sample question and answer she'd written. It was a dramatic reading that—if she did say so herself—put Katie Couric to shame. Her heart was pounding so hard when she was finished she was sure they could all hear it. But when she looked up, they weren't gaping at her chest. They were staring at her face.

Mr. Miniver was nearly chirping.

"What do you think, gang?" he said.

They all looked at Lance.

Don't answer! Lily wanted to shout. *I'll just leave!* She lowered her eyes and started to fold up her proposal.

"You didn't really write that yourself, right?" Lance said. "You got it out of a magazine, didn't you?"

Lily's eyes came up with a jerk. "No!" she said. "This really happened, and I just wrote it up!"

"No, you did not!" the girl named KJ said. She tossed her hair.

"Yes, I did," Lily said, straightening her shoulders. "And I really don't like being called a liar." She wanted to add, *even if you are eighth graders,* but she bit that back. She could tell Lance was getting ready to pounce.

"So say you did write it," he said. "Who's gonna ask a seventh grader for advice?"

Crystal giggled. "Another seventh grader."

"Dude," Doug said. "Readers don't have to know she's in seventh."

"Like they're not gonna know!" KJ said. "How many Lilys are there in this school?"

She flung the hair over her shoulder again as if she wished there were none, but Doug was shaking his big head at her.

"So she doesn't use her own name. We put some kinda fake name on there."

"A pseudonym," Mr. Miniver said.

"Wait—we learned that in science!" Crystal said.

"No, airhead," KJ said. "That was pseudopod."

"So—we could do that pseudo-name thing?" Lance said.

"I don't see why not," Mr. Miniver said. "Any suggestions for what to use?"

Lily raised her hand. She was beginning to feel like she wasn't even in the room anymore—and this was her idea!

"Yes, Lily Pad?" Mr. Miniver said.

"I'd like to be called Answer Girl," she said.

"That's boring!" KJ said.

"Too generic," Lance said.

Crystal nodded.

But Doug turned around and looked at Lily. It was an odd moment to realize that he seemed to have one big thick black eyebrow instead of two, but Lily did. He crunched the big brow in the middle.

"I like it," he said.

"Yeah, but what guy is gonna write in to get advice from a girl?" Lance said.

"Ha!" KJ said. "You guys oughta be asking us girls more. You'd be a lot smarter if you did, right girls?"

Crystal and the other two girls nodded.

"That is SO not true," Lance said.

"And it is SO not on the subject!" Mr. Miniver said. "What do you say, Lance? It's ultimately your decision."

"What does *ultimately* mean?" Crystal said.

"It means I'm the man and what I say goes," Lance said. He swept his sizzling eyes over everybody except Lily. "Okay," he said finally. "We try it in the first issue, and if it stinks, we drop it."

"Fair enough," Mr. Miniver said.

Lily raised her hand. Almost to a person, they rolled their eyes.

"Yeah, what is it?" Lance said. "We gotta talk about features before the bell rings."

"I just want to say that you can be sure it isn't going to stink," Lily said. "In fact, it isn't even going to smell a little bit. It's going to have the aroma of—"

"Okay, okay, we get it," Lance said. "Dougie—what about sports?"

Lily started to sag again. But as Dougie started in about the story he was going to do on the new football coach, Mr. Miniver caught Lily's eye. His mustache went up with his smile, and he very carefully gave her a "thumbs up" sign. And then it was as if they were having a conversation with their eyes—

You show 'em, Lily Pad, his said.

But you saw the way they treated me!

Don't let them get to you. Just kick some buns.

All right, Lily said, with her eyes, mouth, eyebrows, and everything else she could move. *I WILL!*

After the meeting, Mr. Miniver helped her figure out how they were going to get letters from students for her to answer. They decided to place a mailbox on the counter in the front office, where the secretaries could keep an eye on it and kids wouldn't be so likely to mess around with it.

"So, where can we get a mailbox?" Lily asked.

"You're probably going to have to make one," Mr. Miniver said.

KJ stopped on her way out the door. "But bring it in a garbage bag or something," she said. "So if anybody sees you, they won't know you're the Answer Girl." She couldn't seem to resist punctuating that with some eye rolling, but Lily didn't sag this time. She had Mr. Miniver on her side, and that was all she needed.

"And by the way," Lance said, as he joined KJ at the door. "Don't tell any of your little friends you're the Answer Girl. Seventh-grade girls can't keep their mouths shut about anything. It'll be all over the school in, like, ten minutes."

"You have a sister in seventh grade," KJ said.

"Yeah—but she's, like, mature."

Oh, yeah? Lily thought. *Otto is more mature than Ashley!*

"I'll put a notice in the bulletin tomorrow morning," Mr. Miniver said. "You ought to be getting letters in just a few days." The mustache did its little dance. "Get ready!"

Nobody had to tell her that. Right after school, she parked herself in front of the TV to watch Oprah. By the time Mom got home, she was in her third hour of talk shows and had six pages of notes.

"Uh, since when did we turn into a couch potato?" Mom said, as she scooped up the remote control and snapped off the set.

"Since I became Answer Girl," Lily said. "But, Mom, don't tell anybody, okay? Especially Joe."

"I'd agree to that if I knew what an Answer Girl was," Mom said. "There are more groceries in the car. Bring them in for me, would you?"

"Don't you want to know?" Lily said.

"Yes, but I want to know that the milk isn't going to turn into cottage cheese in the driveway first."

"Hey, Mom, got anything to eat?" Joe said, slamming into the kitchen.

Lily stormed out to the car. *This is worse than a newspaper staff meeting!* she thought, as she flung open the van door and caught a bag of canned goods as it headed for the ground. Why is it that nobody listens to me—ever?

Later up in her room, she broke out the journal and a pink gel pen. "God," she wrote, "I never get a minute with Mom. I really want to tell her what I get to do for the paper and why I have to watch talk shows—to get ideas—and there's always somebody around like Joe who would just make fun of me. Besides, this is supposed to be a secret. You're probably the only one I can actually tell!"

She went on until suppertime, and she did feel better. Still, there was the problem of what to do about the Girlz. They already knew about the advice column—but what if one of them blabbed it by mistake? Zooey was a likely candidate for that—or even Kresha when she got excited.

But if Lily was going to keep it a secret, that meant lying to the Girlz—and that was no good. Not only would it break a pact they all had with each other, but also God would hate it.

She still wasn't any closer to an answer when Reni called that night. For once, Lily was happy to hear her rattle on about her new violin piece, and she kept asking her questions about it. But Reni stopped after the third time Lily said, "So tell me some more," and said, "No, your turn. What happened at the newspaper meeting?"

Lily plucked at Otto's fur. He gave her a dirty-dog look and retreated under the bed. She started on China's.

"They won't let me be a reporter," she said.

"Duh! But what about the advice column? Do you get to do it?"

"They liked the idea," Lily said slowly.

"Yeah? And?"

"But they didn't think anybody would want to write for advice from a seventh grader."

"Those slime balls!" Reni said. "They just don't know you, Lily. You're way smarter than any of them. If I need advice, you're the one I go to first!"

"You're prejudiced," Lily said. "So—what about State? Do you get to go?"

"Tryouts aren't for a while," Reni said. "That gives me time to really practice and get good."

"You're already good! I can't believe how good you play for practically just starting!"

"Yeah, well—"

Lily was relieved that they got through most of the rest of the conversation without getting back to the advice column. Until, as they were about to hang up, Reni said, "They just better not let somebody else write that column. It was your idea. You, like, own it."

Then she said she had to go practice, and they said good-bye. Lily hung up with trails of guilt forming in her head.

You let her think you aren't writing it, she told herself. *That's as bad as lying.*

Lily shook her head and whistled for Otto to come out. She needed somebody to talk to or her own inside voice would drive her loony. It was weird how it sounded like Mrs. Reinhold.

By the next morning before school, the rest of the Girlz already knew—from Reni—about the staff "turning down" Lily's column. Reni wasn't there—she was in the orchestra room practicing—but Suzy, Kresha, and Zooey were, and they were buzzing like a trio of angry bees.

"That is so not fair!" Zooey said. She hitched up the waist of her pants. "That was so your column—you did it so good!"

"Smack somebody, Lee-Lee!" Kresha said.

"Where did you get that expression?" Suzy said.

Kresha looked puzzled. "I want Lee-Lee smack somebody!" she said, and she slapped her hand around in the air.

"I don't think she's using it as an expression," Zooey said. She pulled up her pants again. "I'd like to hit someone myself. Who do I hit, Lily?"

"Nobody!" Lily said.

But she couldn't go further. If she told them the truth now, then Reni would know she'd lied to her. You couldn't lie to your best friend.

I'll tell Reni, and then I'll tell them, she decided. *I'll write her a Lily-Gram. Yeah, that felt better.*

"Just don't make a big deal out of it, okay?" Lily said.

"You're so mature," Suzy said. Her little brows pulled together, and for a mini-second, Lily thought of Doug's big, furry ones. "I wish I was as smart as you."

"You're in honors classes," Zooey said. "You have to be smart for that. Man—these stupid pants!"

She lifted the hem of her sweater and rolled the waistband of her pants to make it smaller. Kresha patted Zooey's tummy.

"You get skinny, Zooey!" she said.

"That'll be the day," Zooey said.

The bell rang, and once more Lily was saved ... until second period when the daily bulletin was read over the intercom.

"The Middle School Mirror will feature an advice column in the next issue," the eighth-grade class president read. "Write a letter to the Answer Girl about any problem you have, and your answer may appear in her column."

As he went on to give information about the mailbox in the office, Lily tried to will her face not to go blotchy. She knew those red splotches would be a dead giveaway.

But nobody in her second-period class was looking at her. They were all turning to each other, chattering over the rest of the announcements. Their comments ranged from, "That sounds so lame!" to "Oh, man, do I have some stuff to ask her!" To her amazement, several girls ripped pieces of paper out of their binders and started scribbling right away.

Wow, she thought. *I was right. This IS gonna be big.*

She made a silent vow to herself to get some psychology books out of the library and start studying up tonight. Maybe she could even start going to therapy just to get ideas. She forgot about the Lily-Gram to Reni until she got to her locker before English class and found a neatly folded note, which somebody had slid in the vent.

"Dear Lily," it said in handwriting that was too perfect to belong to anybody but Suzy. "I don't know what a Lily-Gram is but I guess it's some kind of note, so here's mine. I really need to talk to you. You always know so much about everything, and that's what I need. When can we meet? I wish we still met at the Clubhouse every day. I miss that. Why does everything have to change?"

Lily pushed aside her memories of their Girlz Only meetings in the little clubhouse in Reni's backyard. They'd met there for all of sixth grade. Right now she felt as if she were small enough to fit into it again. She'd forgotten all about Suzy wanting to talk to her, and she hadn't said a word about it that morning at the bench.

I'm the worst friend on the planet, she thought. *I'm gonna talk to her right away.*

She snatched what she needed from the locker and walked as fast as she dared past the teacher on hall duty to get to Mrs. Reinhold's classroom. She was going to set up a time to get together with Suzy. It was going to be more important than anything else ... until she got there. Reni was already hanging at the doorway, and Lily could almost see her blowing steam out of her nose like an angry bull.

"Lily!" she said, brown eyes blazing. "Did you hear that announcement this morning?"

"Um, yeah," Lily said.

"We have to do something about that! We have to do something big!"

"No!" Lily cried.

"But they stole your idea!" Reni said. "That's so not fair!"

"It's okay," was all Lily could think to say. Her mind was racing, but it wasn't getting anywhere.

"It is SO not okay!"

"Ladies." It was, of course, Mrs. Reinhold, cobwebs in full motion. "I didn't think it was necessary to tell you that I don't allow screaming like banshees outside my classroom."

Lily was about to apologize, but Reni was too quick for her.

"You don't understand," she said to Mrs. Reinhold. "Those stupid newspaper people wouldn't let Lily do the advice column, when it was her idea, and now they're doing it!"

Mrs. Reinhold looked at her blankly. "And this has what to do with you, Reni?"

"Well—duh—like everything!"

" 'Duh'?" Mrs. Reinhold said. "Define that for me."

Lily was ready to climb into her own backpack and zip it up. Reni, it appeared, was just getting started.

"I don't mean to be disrespectful or anything," she said, "but you don't know how it is with me and Lily—"

"Lily and me—"

"But if something evil happens to her, it's like it's happening to me too, and the same way with her."

Reni looked at Lily, who nodded woodenly. *Only you're so much better than me,* Lily thought. *I'm lying to you right this very minute.*

"I certainly admire your loyalty," Mrs. Reinhold said. "So why don't you do something about it?"

Lily froze.

"Like what?" Reni asked.

Mrs. Reinhold adjusted her tiny glasses. "Perhaps, Reni, you should write a letter to the editor of the *Mirror*. You're a fairly decent writer, though you'll want me to edit for spelling." Her mouth turned up at only one corner. "You're rather a creative speller."

"What good would that do?" Reni said. "I'm just asking."

"The way it's supposed to work is that they receive your letter and then they print it in the paper—"

"No!" Lily said.

Mrs. Reinhold's glasses nearly fell off her nose, and Reni stared at Lily, bunchy mouth gaping. Lily decided later that God must really like her, because the bell rang just then.

"You're not going to count us tardy are you?" Reni said. "Since we were talking to you?"

Lily couldn't have cared less. She'd have been overjoyed, in fact, if Mrs. Reinhold had just sent her home—forever.

All through class, all she could do was chew on her pencil. Sentences where she was supposed to choose the correct pronouns made no sense at all as she stared at them, gnawing on her eraser. What difference did it make whether she used he or him, now that the whole newspaper staff was going to know what a blabbermouth she was? She went back and forth in her head—if I tell Reni the truth, then I have to lie to the staff; if I don't tell her, and she sends a letter, they'll probably kick me out for not keeping the secret. By the time the bell rang, she had eaten the eraser and was starting on the metal part.

She decided she had to avoid Reni as much as she could until she'd made a decision. After class, she told her to go on to geography so she could talk to Mrs. Reinhold, and then she dawdled until ten seconds before the bell and slipped into her seat unnoticed by the frazzled Ms. Ferringer. During the lecture on the Mediterranean Coast, she wrote Reni a Lily-Gram: "Have to go to newspaper room at lunch. See you after school."

The newspaper room was actually the last place she wanted to go. She wasn't sure she could handle the eye rolling and the hair tossing today. But when she got there, nobody was tossing or rolling. They were bent over something in the middle of the room, all chattering at once.

"Dude, it's only been like three hours and we already got this many!"

"This is awesome!"

"I wanna read some—"

"No—this is Lily's project." Mr. Miniver glanced up and broke into a twinkly smile. "Here's the girl of the hour now!"

"Hey, look at this," Doug said. He hoisted the mailbox up and tilted it her way. It was half full of folded pieces of paper.

"I'm glad you're the one doing this, and not me," KJ said, giving the inevitable toss. "I don't see how you're even going to have time to read them all, much less answer them."

Lily approached slowly, her eyes glued to the box. "Are those all for me?"

"Well, duh," Lance said. "I don't think people are putting letters to the president in there."

Crystal pulled out a handful and flipped through them. "They all say 'To Answer Girl' on them."

"Yikes," Lily said.

"Now, before you panic," Mr. Miniver said, "the way we'll do this is we'll go through and select the best ones—the ones that will appeal to the most readers. We'll only print and answer those."

"So can we start reading them?" KJ said.

Mr. Miniver looked at Lily.

What does she mean "we"? she said to him with her eyes.

Leave it to me, his mustache said back.

"I don't remember this being a group effort," he said to the rest of the staff. "I think you all need to work on your own stories."

"Yeah," Lance said. He hadn't spoken until now, and Lily noticed he alone didn't look terribly jazzed. In fact, his lip was in mid-curl.

Lily didn't give him a chance to curl it at her. She sat right down at the table next to Mr. Miniver and started to read. Within seconds, it wouldn't have mattered if the rest of the staff had staged a protest march, she wouldn't have noticed. The letters were intriguing.

Some of them were obviously somebody's attempt at a sense of humor.

Dear Answer Girl,

What do I do about a cat that always pees on my homework?

Dear Answer Girl,

Could I get a disease from sharing a gym locker with somebody?

Others were serious but, as even Mr. Miniver agreed, lame.

Dear Answer Girl,

Do you think it's fair that a teacher doesn't give you an A even if you're trying as hard as you can?

Dear Answer Girl,

Why do we have to have stupid little seventh graders in this school anyway? Do you know a way we could make it all eighth graders?

Still others were "just somebody showing off," Mr. Miniver said.

Dear Answer Girl,

I think your column is a lame idea. What are you gonna do about that?

Dear Answer Girl,

Drop dead!

Mr. Miniver crumpled those up and tossed them into the trash can like he was making a basket.

"You know, Lily Pad," he said, "you can set the tone for the future of your column by the letters you choose to answer this first time. If you give any of that kind the time of day, you're setting yourself up for more of the same."

"Yeah," Lily said slowly. "But I don't want it to be all serious. I think we need some fun ones."

"Good thinking."

So they selected only two, since Lily said that was usually how many there were in the "Dear Abby" column. She'd been reading it every day like it was a textbook.

Dear Answer Girl,

I can never get my locker open. I'm always forgetting the combination, and it's always, like, when I'm late for class or have to go to the bathroom. Help!
—Locked Out

Dear Answer Girl,

I have this teacher who makes fun of me almost every day in front of the whole class. I don't want to give you the details, because then he'll know who I am, but it's so embarrassing. Now the other kids in class are starting to do it too, and he never stops them. What do I do?

—Red Face

"Good choices," Mr. Miniver said.

The rest of the staff grudgingly agreed when he read them out loud, although after pawing through the box, Doug said he liked the one about the cat peeing on the homework better.

"When should I have my answers ready?" Lily said.

Lance grunted. "All deadlines are Monday."

"Does that give you enough time?" Mr. Miniver said.

KJ gave a toss. "That's when the rest of us have to have ours in."

"Then I will too," Lily said.

Mr. Miniver's eyes were approving. Everyone else's said, *I seriously doubt it.*

Lily swung her backpack on and started for the door, but out of the corner of her eye, she caught Mr. Miniver watching her. When she turned toward him, his face plainly told her, *Don't let them get to you, Lily Pad.*

So Lily stopped. She looked back at the staff, who were all curling and rolling and tossing, and she smiled.

"I'll probably have them done by tomorrow," she said. Using her best model's pivot, she changed directions and strolled out the door.

It felt good, until she heard KJ say, "I bet her answers are going to be so lame."

Lily didn't stop, and she didn't turn. *I am SO going to show them,* she thought, teeth gritting. *They're gonna eat my dust.*

Although how she was going to pull that off, she wasn't quite sure. Sitting in her room that night, after watching several talk shows and going through a couple of psychology books Dad had in his study and discussing the issue with Otto and China, all she could do was stare at the blank sheet of paper in front of her. There were several crumpled up ones on the floor—or at least the remains of them. Otto had thought they were for him, and he'd growled ferociously as he'd torn them to shreds.

So far, everything she'd come up with had been lame just as KJ had predicted.

But I can't let her be right! Lily thought. *I just can't!*

She flopped back against China with a sigh. "Why did I ever think I could do this?" she said to Otto, who was looking longingly at her pen and licking his little gray chops. "It's all Marcie McCleary's fault. She said I gave the best advice."

Gnawing on the end of her green gel pen, she thought back to that incident with Marcie. All Lily had said to her was, "So don't turn around." But Marcie's problem had been so easy. It was just what Mom called "using your head for something besides your hat."

"I just told Marcie what I'd have done if it was me," she said to Otto. "This is different. This is writing—for the whole school!"

But since Otto didn't come up with anything better, she looked at the first question again.

"I can never get my locker open."

"What would I do if it were me?" Lily muttered. "Duh! It is me!" *I hear you,* she wrote. *I've had so many problems with my locker, I'm thinking of going after it with a hammer—a big hammer. But since they'll write you up for that—like about a thousand other things, in case you haven't noticed—I suggest this: paint the numbers to your locker combination on your fingernails with nail polish. That way they'll always be there. Now, if you're a boy, that could be a little bit of a problem, but come on, are you in touch with your feminine side or not?*

"What do you think of this, Otto?" she said.

Lily read it out loud to him. When she looked up for his response, she found him chewing off the business end of her green gel pen. She grabbed it just before it squirted out onto the bedspread, but ended up with about half the ink on her hand.

"Oh, man!" she said.

She raced toward the bathroom, but Joe was in there taking a bath and screamed for her not to come in under threat of being assaulted with a flying bar of soap.

She tore down the stairs toward the kitchen and almost collided head on with Art, who was emerging with a sandwich big enough for three people.

"New trend?" he asked, nodding at the ink. "What you seventh graders won't come up with next!"

Lily went for the sink. "Like you were never a seventh grader," she said.

"Yeah, about a hundred years ago."

"Four years."

"So who's counting?" he said, his mouth full of salami and rye. "Besides, I'm a lot more savvy than I was back then."

"What does savvy mean?" Lily said.

Art leaned against the doorframe and licked off the mustard that had leaked out onto his fingers. "Streetwise. You know—like I know how to solve problems I didn't back then."

Lily looked up from her soapy hands, and she could feel the gleam coming into her eyes. "Okay," she said, "so how would you solve this: somebody's got a teacher that makes fun of him. Now the other kids in the class are doing it too. What does he do?"

Art chewed thoughtfully.

"I mean, I'd go straight to the principal," Lily said.

"Nah—too nerdy. No offense, but that's just gonna make things worse."

"Yeah, I guess."

Art narrowed his eyes at her. "You're not talking about yourself, are you?"

"No!" Lily said. "It's somebody else. I just wondered what you'd do."

"Why?"

"Because you just said you were savvy."

"No, I mean, what difference does it make to you?"

Lily stiffened. *I can't even tell my brother. This is, like, major hard.*

"Never mind," Art said. "I forgot you and your little friends were into crying on each other's shoulders. Oh, by the way, that one chick called again while I was on the phone. I got her on call waiting and told her you'd call her back, but she said no."

"She didn't say who she was?"

Art shook his head as he stuffed the last of the sandwich into his mouth. His cheeks bulged.

"That is so weird," Lily said. "I don't think any of the Girlz would do that."

"Tell him not to set himself up to be laughed at."

"Who?" Lily said.

"The kid with the teacher that's making fun of him. Tell him not to walk around cringing like he's waiting for somebody to attack. Tell him to sit in his desk like he owns the room and dare anybody to hassle him—not with words, though—with his eyes."

"Wow," Lily said. She watched him as she absently dried her hands. "How did you think of that?"

"That's how I got through seventh grade," Art said. "I was the little band geek, remember?" He made a goofy face.

"Oh, yeah," Lily said. "You had buck teeth."

"B.B.," he said.

"Huh?"

"Before braces."

Art went to the refrigerator muttering, "Dude, I'm still hungry," and Lily took the steps two at a time up to her room.

"I never thought I'd say this," she told Otto as she searched for another pen, "but I am so glad I have an older brother."

Otto gave a low growl and went back to sleep, curled up against China. Lily squeezed in there too and began to write.

Dear Red Face,

First of all, that is the biggest bummer on the planet. If I didn't think it was nerdy, I'd tell you to go straight to the principal. But since that would only make things worse, give this a shot. Don't walk into the classroom slinking against the wall like you're just waiting for somebody to come after you. Walk in like you own the place, and sit in your desk that way too. After all, where do they get off putting you down—and especially a teacher! Look around the room that way too, and dare anybody, including the teacher, to give you a hard time. I'm thinking it could take a day or two, but if you don't let them think they can win, they'll probably give it up. If not, then go ahead and be a nerd. Write an anonymous letter to the principal. Meanwhile, remember who you are.

"I like that last line the best," Lily said to the sleeping Otto. "You know what? This is pretty good."

But as she turned out the light and snuggled in beside Otto, she couldn't help but wonder if the rest of the staff would think so.

You oughta pray about it, she told herself.

But she was too tired to get up and get out her prayer journal.

I'll send him a God-Gram, she thought sleepily.

God—make them like it, would you? I don't want to see any more rolling eyes.

First thing the next morning, Lily went straight to the newspaper room and gave Mr. Miniver her answers.

"I'll pass them on to Lance," he said. "I see him first period."

"Then what happens?" Lily said.

"He makes any changes he feels are necessary, and it becomes part of the layout."

"Changes?" Lily said. The idea of Lance doing anything to her answers made her hand itch to snatch back the paper.

But Mr. Miniver smiled, mustache and all. "Don't worry, Lily Pad," he said. "Everything has to be approved by me."

Then his twinkly eyes added, *I won't let him mess it up.*

Lily twinkled her thanks and headed out to the bench to meet the Girlz.

But as she hurried down the steps, checking twice to make sure she was on the set that was designated DOWN, not UP, a nagging feeling started in her stomach, and she slowed her pace.

What if Reni were there? In all the hustle to get her answers written, she'd totally forgotten that she had to do something about Reni before she wrote a letter to the editor, and Lily still had no idea what.

And what about Suzy? Lily still hadn't managed to find time to talk to her. In fact, she realized with an even naggier feeling, she hadn't even remembered Suzy until right this minute.

They'll understand, she thought. Last summer, they were all too busy for me. Maybe it's just my turn to have important stuff to do.

Still, her head was full of "I'm sorrys" as she swung off the stairs and went for the bench. She breathed a sigh of relief. Only Kresha and Zooey were there.

"Hey, Lily, listen to this!" Zooey said, bobbing her head at Kresha, ponytail topknot flopping, bangs dancing. "Go ahead, Kresh. Say it to her."

Kresha grinned, her own set of bangs hanging over her eyebrows. "Good morning, Li-ly."

Lily stared at her. "You said it right!"

"No more 'Lee-Lee'!" Zooey said. "Course, I thought it was kinda cute when she used to say it that way."

"No!" Kresha said, a frown making a "W" on her forehead. "I do not talk cute anymore!"

"You sound so American!" Lily said.

Kresha's "W" disappeared, and she threw her arms around Lily's neck and deposited a kiss on each of her cheeks. The Girlz were used to Kresha doing stuff like that, but Lily still looked around to make sure no one was watching. It got a little embarrassing sometimes.

"What else can you say?" Lily said as she untangled herself from Kresha.

The "W" reappeared. "I can say—why they not let you write ad-vice."

"Uh—that should be 'why didn't they let you write advice,'" Lily said quickly.

Zooey looked up from rolling the waistband of her jeans. "Yeah, why didn't they?" she said.

"Why are all your pants too big all of a sudden?" Lily said.

Zooey shrugged. "I guess they're all stretching out."

"No," Kresha said. "Zooey—Zooey is skinny."

"I don't think so!" Zooey said. But her round face was beaming.

Lily was happy for the change in subject. Until the warning bell rang, she made sure they talked about Zooey's new measurements and the new clothes she was going to have to buy if she kept losing weight.

Lily couldn't help but wonder where Suzy was as she fought her way through the crowd to Mrs. Reinhold's classroom. Reni, she figured, was in the orchestra room practicing. But Suzy never missed a Girlz meeting. Once Suzy thought there was a rule, she'd rather die than break it.

Suzy, it turned out, was already in the room when Lily got there. She had her head down on her folded arms on the top of the desk. Glancing warily at the clock, Lily went over to her and squatted down.

"Suzy?" she said. "You okay?"

Suzy nodded without raising her head. "Just tired," she said into her folded arms.

"You sure?"

Another nod, and then the bell rang. Lily wasn't in her seat.

She sprang up, jack-in-the-box style, as Mrs. Reinhold was closing the door. There was time to get to her desk before the teacher turned around, if Lily took a shortcut.

Dropping to her hands and knees, Lily crawled under Suzy's desk and made for the far row. It was definitely a different view down here—all you could see were shoes. Nikes mostly. Some Sketchers. A loafer here and there. A pair of pumps.

Pumps?

Lily stopped and stared at the trim black shoes set primly in nylons. Nobody wore heels and hose to school. Except Mrs. Reinhold.

Lily's eyes made a slow journey up and over the sensible gray skirt, the no-nonsense white turtleneck, the pointy nose, and the teeny-weeny glasses. Mrs. Reinhold adjusted them with the tips of her index fingers, magnifying her eyes—her very not-pleased eyes.

Lily tried to scramble up, and hit her head soundly on someone's desktop. There was no time to nurse it, though. She got to her feet and shoved her hair out of her face.

"What on earth were you doing?" Mrs. Reinhold said.

There was a general snicker in the room, which she silenced with a stony stare.

"I didn't want you to see that I wasn't in my seat," Lily said.

There were more snickers, and this time Mrs. Reinhold ignored them. She was too busy squinting at Lily, as if she were trying to see inside her head.

"You're nothing if not honest," Mrs. Reinhold said. "Go on to your place—and use your feet to get there."

Lily's face had by this time skipped blotchy and gone straight on to bright red. Nobody was making any attempt to smother the giggles, snickers, and the out-and-out jeers this go-around.

No—let me crawl! she thought miserably. *Right out the door!*

Why, she wondered in agony as she neared her seat and kept her eyes deliberately away from Ashley, didn't Mrs. Reinhold stop them all from laughing at her? What was up with that?

Then she stopped, two steps short of her desk. There was something familiar about this. She could almost hear Art saying, *Tell him not to walk around cringing like he's waiting for somebody to attack. Tell him to sit in his desk like he owns the room and dare anybody to hassle him—not with words, though—with his eyes.*

Lily straightened her shoulders and lifted her chin. Easing her backpack from her shoulders she dropped it neatly onto the back of her chair. Then she turned around and swept the room with a look she hoped said, *Is there a problem here? I'm fairly certain this is MY classroom.*

"Ooh!" Chelsea said, and then slapped her hand over her mouth and pretended to be looking for something in her purse.

While Mrs. Reinhold was fixing her stony stare on Chelsea, Lily slipped into her desk and looked around once more. Most of the class was still watching her, faces a little bewildered.

I dare you to snicker one more time, she said with her eyes. *I double-dog dare you.*

A few scratched their heads. A couple of others exchanged glances. But nobody rolled an eye or tossed a hairdo.

Except Ashley. When Lily looked at her, she did both. But she didn't say a word when Lily stared her down. She just flounced herself around to face front again.

Trying to smother a smile, Lily got busy underlining subordinate clauses.

It was hard to keep a smile off her face as she concentrated on straight shoulders and a gaze that read, *Don't mess with me. I don't cringe anymore.*

When it was time to take her bag lunch into the newspaper room, however, her courage faded a little. Lance was, as usual, sitting on the edge of Mr. Miniver's desk, scowling at her Answer Girl paper. Lily looked around.

"Where's Mr. Miniver?" she said.

"Down in the cafeteria getting some lunch," Crystal said. She was sitting at a computer, staring at the screen and biting her nails.

"Is he coming back?"

"I don't know."

Lily looked anxiously at Lance again. "He's always in here during lunch, right?"

"I guess!" Crystal jerked around in her chair. "I'm trying to get this stupid story done—do you mind?"

Lily felt herself starting to sag, but she lined her shoulders up again and, dropping her backpack onto a table, marched right up to Lance.

"So—" she said, "what do you think?"

Lance didn't look at her. "You should of used a colon after 'shot.'"

"A colon?" Lily said. She was fighting to keep the I-dare-you-to-hassle-me look in her eyes. "We haven't gotten to those yet in grammar."

"You got Mrs. Reinhold?' said a voice behind her.

Lily looked up and nodded in the direction of Doug's big eyebrow.

"Then you will."

"I thought a colon was part of your intestine," Crystal said.

"And I thought you had an article to finish," Lance said.

"Oh, yeah," Crystal said, and she swiveled back around, head ducked.

You shouldn't cringe, Crystal, Lily thought. *Then Lance wouldn't pick on you.*

Lily tilted her chin at him now. "Anything else?" she said.

Lance glowered at the paper again, and Lily studied him carefully. His sizzling, blue eyes went up and down the thing at least four times. But in the end, he had to shake his head.

"I guess not," he said.

Over at the layout table, KJ gave a loud grunt.

"What's the matter with you?" Doug said.

"Why does she just get one little comment about a punctuation mark and that's all? You tear everybody else's stuff apart." As Lily expected, KJ flipped a trail of tendrils over her shoulder. "I mean—she's a seventh grader."

Everyone looked at Lily as if they expected her to answer the question. She looked back at them, heart hammering, but eyes telling them to back off.

"If there's nothing for him to tear apart," Lily said, "what's he supposed to do?"

"Score!" Doug said.

"Shut up," KJ said, bending over the table again.

"Oh, there will be none of that here," Mr. Miniver said from the doorway.

Lily couldn't help being relieved. Acting brave was okay; not having to was better.

"What's the verdict, Lance?" Mr. Miniver said, nodding at Lily's paper.

Lance shrugged. "It's okay."

"Just okay?" KJ said. "I thought everything we did was supposed to be 'top quality.' "

"Our 'okay' is top quality," Mr. Miniver said. "There you go, Lily. Type it up."

Lily took her paper and headed for a computer, chin up, shoulders straight. Yeah, this was feeling good.

Once the piece was done, it was still five days before the newspaper would come out. During that time, the staff gave Lily every piece of "grunt work" they could come up with—correcting spelling on other people's pieces, running to the supply room for printer cartridges and packs of paper, sharpening all the pencils on the reporters' shelf. The more Lily held her own, the more mindless things they found for her to do.

Except for Doug. He asked her to help him find different ways to give the football scores so they wouldn't all sound the same. Several times he gave her his stuff before he handed it in to Lance, just to make sure it "didn't sound dumb." And whenever KJ rolled her eyes at Lily or Lance reminded her she was a seventh grader, Doug pretended to toss his hair or curled his lip. That always helped Lily knock Lance and KJ and the rest of them back with an "is-there-a-problem?" look.

The day she nearly got knocked back herself, though, was the day Lance dumped a handful of papers in front of her and told her to enter them on the computer because they were going in the next issue. The one on top was from Reni.

Dear Editor,

I think it's so unfair that when a seventh grader, Lily Robbins, suggested an advice column, you wouldn't let her be the one to write it—just because she isn't in eighth grade. They call that discrimination—and you shouldn't be allowed to do it.

—Reni Johnson

Lily's stomach felt like it was completely turning over. She glanced up at Lance, but he was busy reaming Crystal out about the "lame" article she'd turned in. Obviously, he hadn't even read the letter, or he would have said something. Lily would have been out of here on her ear already.

Then if he hasn't read it, said a voice from a dark corner of her mind, *he'll never miss it if it doesn't make it into the paper.*

Willing herself not to "spaz out," Lily slid the letter into her lap. After another cautious glance around the room at the heads all bent over their work, she dropped it into the trash can.

Once the letter was disposed of, at least one problem was solved. She didn't have to avoid Reni anymore—and that would have been a happy thing if now that she wanted to see her there was ever a chance. She realized that almost the only contact she had with Reni was trading Lily-Grams. Reni practiced every morning before school in the orchestra room, and whenever she could get her work done before the end of a class, she headed down there. Except in Mrs. Reinhold's class, of course. She didn't even ask in there.

"Miss you," Lily wrote one day. "Can you spend the night Friday?"

"Not this Friday," Reni wrote back. "You—my house—next Friday?"

"Yeah."

The other thing Lily had to think about was Suzy. She got to school just before the bell rang every day, so she missed the bench action.

When Lily finally did remember to write her a Lily-Gram that said "What's wrong?" Suzy wrote back, "My mom brings me now."

That explained why Suzy was just under the wire every day. Her dad had always dropped her off on his way to work so her mom could take her other sisters to their schools. But it didn't answer the "what's wrong" question. And there was never a chance to try to pry it out of her. Since she didn't come before school, Lily went to the newspaper room during lunch, and Art pretty much hogged the phone at home—*when am I supposed to talk to her?* Lily thought. Middle school was so much more demanding than elementary. At least there they had recess.

But Kresha and Zooey joined Lily every morning, and they certainly didn't have problems. Kresha was so proud of how well she was learning English, she babbled and gurgled almost the entire time. Zooey started appearing in new clothes, and Kresha all but broke out a tape measure to show how much weight Zooey was losing.

"Are you eating?" Lily said.

"Like a truck driver!" Zooey said. "My mom says it's the PE class. She was gonna call the teacher and complain that it was too hard for me, but I'm starting to like it. Guess how many sit-ups I can do!"

Then she proceeded to drop to the cement and execute several, while her round cheeks went red immediately. Lily secretly hoped she wouldn't lose those. Then she wouldn't even look like Zooey anymore.

It's just like Suzy said in her Lily-Gram, Lily wrote in her journal that night. *Everything's changing—and why does it have to? I liked things the way they were before—with the Clubhouse and all.*

She thought of God and added—*Please, Lord, could you slow things down a little?*

But God didn't answer that God-Gram. In fact, even more things were about to change—big time.

On newspaper day, Lily got to leave fourth period early so she could help distribute papers to classes before lunch. It was all she could do not to grab one off the top of her stack and turn right to the "Answer Girl" column before she started just to see how it looked in print.

But Lance had impressed on them how important it was for them to hurry so that it all got done. As she was leaving the staff room, Mr. Miniver whispered to her, "Good job, Lily! It looks great!" She had never been so grateful for his exclamation points.

Passing out the bundles of papers to teachers turned out to be fun—well, mostly. In one math class—which reminded Lily more of a zoo than a classroom—there were three boys to every girl, and every one of them had some comment to make when Lily entered the room.

"Hey, Baby!"

"Dude—where'd you get the hair?"

"Man, is that real? Lemme see if that's real!"

"Don't worry about it, Lily," she heard somebody whisper.

Lily looked down to see Zooey in the desk beside her.

"They do that to everybody who comes in here," Zooey said.

But Lily wasn't worried about it. She gave them all her "who-died-and-left-you-bunch-of-zoo-animals-in-charge?" look. That silenced all the voices—except one.

"Ooh, Snobbins," Shad Shifferdecker said. "You think you're all bad now or somethin'?"

Lily refused to look at him. If anybody could rattle her cage, it was Shad, no matter how tough she was getting.

Instead, she looked around for the teacher. Shad wasn't giving up that easily. As she was craning her neck for sight of somebody who was supposedly in charge, he leapfrogged several desks and planted himself right in front of her.

"So I hear you think you're all that now," he said.

"Really?" she said. She was willing her face not to go blotchy, and she kept her eyes sweeping the room for a teacher.

"Yeah. Well, dream on."

"There's no need to dream, Shad," she said. "I already woke up from my nightmare—because you're not in any of my classes."

"Busted!" one of the boys shouted.

"You lose, Shifferdecker!" said another one.

"Oh, hi," said still another voice. A curly-haired teacher who didn't look a whole lot older than Art waved to Lily from where she sat on the floor against the wall next to a student who was peering into a basic math book. "Just leave them on the desk," the teacher said cheerfully—as if the Bronx Zoo wasn't all around her.

"She so did not bust me," Lily heard Shad protesting as she dumped the papers on the desk and got out the door. "Snobbins is weird."

At least Lily's face waited until she got out into the hall to blotch up. *Why is it he can get to me when nobody else can anymore?*

But by the end of lunch, Shad was the furthest thing from her mind. The *Mirror* staff was allowed to take the period off, and Lily ate with the Girlz—except Reni, who was, of course, in the orchestra room practicing. At least Lily wouldn't have to pretend to be concerned when Reni noticed that her letter hadn't made it into the paper.

Reni would have too, because it seemed like everybody in the cafeteria was either reading the paper or talking about it. Most of what they were saying was about the "Answer Girl."

"This is funny—"

"I totally love these answers. I'm gonna write to her—"

"I bet they got this out of a magazine—"

"Nuh-uh—I know the girl that wrote the question. She showed it to me before she turned it in—"

The Girlz, however, were not impressed.

"It's okay," Zooey said. "But you could have done it better, Lily."

"That's right," Suzy said.

The nagging feeling started in Lily's stomach. "You're just saying that because you're my best friends," she said. "Aren't you?"

Suzy hesitated, but Zooey and Kresha were shaking their heads with a vengeance.

"I thought Reni was gonna write a letter to the auditor," Zooey said.

"Editor," Suzy corrected her.

"They don't all get in," Lily said. At least it wasn't a lie.

Comments about the "Answer Girl" continued all through fifth period until Mr. Chester said if he heard one more word about it, they were all getting double homework. Nobody believed him, although Reni did agree in a loud voice. She wrote Lily a Lily-Gram: "Sorry about column. Guess my letter didn't help."

The other note Lily got during that class was one an office aide delivered from Mr. Miniver.

"Come see me after school!" he had written in a big scrawling print. "It's important!"

When the final bell rang, she made tracks for the newspaper room. The whole staff was there, sitting on the long table. They were all grinning—except, of course, for Lance, but even he wasn't curling his lip. Mr. Miniver's mustache was nearly out of control.

"Come over here, Lily Pad!" he said. "We have something to show you!"

"What?" Lily said. She approached them slowly. There was something strange about the way they were all smiling at her.

"Come see for yourself!"

Doug hopped down off the table, reached behind everybody, and lifted up the full "Answer Girl" mailbox. "We can't even count how many letters we've gotten since fourth period," he said.

"There must be like two thousand!" Crystal said.

KJ cowed her with a look. "We don't even have two thousand people in the whole school," she said.

"Maybe some people wrote two."

"Maybe you're a moron," KJ said.

Lily continued to grin. "Is that whole box full of letters?"

"Yeah," Doug said. "And that on the table's the overflow."

"Looks like 'Answer Girl' is a big hit," Mr. Miniver said.

"So I say we make it bigger," Lance said.

Lily stared at him. *All right,* she wanted to say. *Who are you and what have you done with our editor?*

"Do, like, ten questions this time," he said.

"We don't want to wear out a good thing," Mr. Miniver said. "But I'd agree to four."

"You can do four, can't you?" KJ said.

Lily tossed her hair back. "Sure," she said. "I'll do as many as you want."

"Dude, how do you do that?" Doug said.

"She's like this genius or something," Crystal said.

"Uh, talk about overdoing a good thing," Lance said. But his lip remained uncurled. His blue eyes sizzled at Lily, only they didn't burn. They said, *Okay, so maybe you're not such a geek after all.*

"Then we better get started, Lily Pad," Mr. Miniver said, pointing to the box. "The deadline is a week from today."

"For everybody?" Crystal said.

"No, Crystal," Lance said. "You're special. We're giving you until next year."

Crystal drooped.

"Don't do that," Lily said to her when Lance had moved away.

"Do what?"

"Act like you're afraid of him. It's like I said in the column—dare him with your eyes to hassle you like that."

"Wow," Crystal said. "You really are smart." She glanced cautiously around the room. "Would you help me with my story this time?"

"Sure," Lily said. "No problem."

Crystal wasn't the only one who hit on her for assistance. Over the next several days, as the stories were assigned, Doug and a couple of other kids came to Lily for suggestions. That meant she had to do most of her own writing at home, but that was okay.

"Nobody can really help me with mine," she told Otto. She tapped her forehead. "It's all up here."

She and Mr. Miniver had chosen two fun questions and two serious ones. The fun ones she whipped out the first night—one on what to do about a kid who sits next to you with breath that would exterminate termites, and the other dealing with a teacher whose voice sounds like a fingernail going down a chalkboard.

The serious ones were harder, but Lily was determined to tough it out. The night she sat down to work on them, she just asked herself: *What would I do in that situation?*

When she did that, the first serious answer practically wrote itself.

Dear Answer Girl,

I feel like such a loser. Nobody notices me. What can I do to get more popular?

—Loser

Dear Loser,

I hope this is the last time anybody calls you that. I've been there—I was a loser at one time myself. But no more, and here's the trick: find out what you're really good at and then go for it, 950 percent! While you're doing it, look everybody in the eye, and I promise you they won't be able to even say the word loser *in your presence.*

But the second one didn't come quite so easily.

Dear Answer Girl,

My best friend doesn't want to hang out with me anymore. He's all popular now, and he acts like he thinks I'm a geek. We used to be like so close. You got any suggestions?

—Ditched

Dear Ditched,

It was as far as Lily got.

"That's never happened to me," she told Otto. "And I can't ask Art this time—'cause I bet it never happened to him either." That was true. Art was always saying that he had turned being a band geek into a serious art form, so now everybody wanted to be one.

An uneasiness settled over Lily. What if she couldn't do this? What if she'd already written the best stuff she had and the rest was going to be lame and everybody on the staff was going to be disappointed and say, "I told you she was just a seventh grader"? There was nobody she could call except somebody on the staff. No way!

Lily's chest hurt. *I wish I could talk to Mom,* she thought. It seemed like it was too late now to tell her about the column. And besides, Mom was always too busy.

She used to always have time for me, and now it's all about her volleyball team and stuff, Lily thought.

She glanced down at the letter. In a way, she did feel the same as "Ditched," only it was like her own mom doing it to her.

"So it is me!" she said to Otto. "What am I doing about it?"

Otto rolled over on his back, feet in the air, and Lily absently scratched his belly.

She'd sort of given up on Mom. *I'm busy with my own life anyway,* she thought. She sat up so abruptly, Otto rolled off the bed.

"That's it!" she said.

He gave her a dark look.

"No—really!"

She pulled the pen out from behind her ear and flipped to a clean sheet of paper.

Dear Ditched,

It's over, Dude. He's got his life—so why don't you get one too? Yeah, it's a bummer when you lose a friend, but this is middle school. Stuff changes.

She stopped writing. Her chest was getting tighter.

"Otto?" she said.

Otto jumped up on the bed and nuzzled at her hand. She pulled him close and hugged him until he started to wiggle.

"Don't change, okay?" she whispered into the top of his wiry-haired head. "Just stay like you are."

He gave her a reassuring bite on the finger. Feeling better, she finished her answer.

When Lily got to third period a few days later, there were two folded pieces of paper on her desk.

One was a Lily-Gram from Suzy, who hadn't shown up at the bench again that morning: "Can we walk to fourth period together?" it said.

The second wasn't a Lily-Gram. It was written in silver gel ink on black paper in round writing with lots of hearts for i-dots and smiley faces at the ends of sentences.

"I'm having a sleepover tonight," Lily read. "You want to come? It's at 6:30. Bring a sleeping bag. Write down who you like on a piece of paper. Ashley A."

Lily stared at it until her eyes ached.

A note from Ashley that didn't say, "You are the biggest nerd in life, and I wouldn't have you at one of my parties if somebody paid me." What was up with that?

It's a trick, Lily thought. *Don't fall for it.*

But there was nothing about the invitation that looked suspicious. If anybody else had left it for her, she wouldn't have given it a doubtful thought. Still—this was Ashley.

Lily studied the black paper again, and that's when she spotted a small arrow at the bottom, indicating that there was more on the back. Steeling herself for the worst, Lily slowly turned it over.

"P.S. My brother thinks you're cool!"

Ashley's brother? Lance?

No way! she told herself. *Don't believe it!*

But she couldn't just toss the thing in the trash. For one thing, Lance hadn't curled his lip at her the day the paper had come out and all those letters had poured in. In fact, he hadn't done it since then. Lily sat up straighter in her chair. After all, she wasn't letting people get to her anymore. It must be working.

"So, are you coming?"

Lily looked up. Ashley and Chelsea were both standing there, smiling in a way that reminded Lily of salesgirls in the Gap saying "May I help you?"

"Um—I don't know," Lily stammered. "I mean—I'd have to ask."

Immediately, she wanted to bite her upper lip off. They were sure to pounce on asking parents' permission as the geekiest practice since playing with Barbies.

But Chelsea continued to smile and said, "Don't you hate that?"

"They'll let you come, though," Ashley said. "If they say no, just go slam your door. My dad always feels guilty when he makes me slam my door, and then he lets me do whatever."

Lily had a clear picture of herself doing that—and being grounded until she was twenty. But she nodded as if she agreed.

"You can turn in who you like to me or Ashley anytime," Chelsea said. "We won't show them to anybody else."

Lily was a little confused, but she didn't want to look that way. Maybe just the right question would clear it up. "How many names can I put down?" she said.

Ashley and Chelsea looked at each other as if Lily had just asked how many millions of dollars she should bring to the party.

"How many boys do you like?" Chelsea said.

"Oh," Lily said. She was glad she'd asked. She'd have written Reni, Suzy, Zooey, and Kresha, and been the laughingstock of the entire school by second period. "I'll just put down my top two," she said, tossing her red hair out of her face.

Ashley and Chelsea exchanged glances again.

"Just write down your top ONE," Ashley said. "Otherwise it won't work."

"What won't?" Lily said.

"We're gonna get a bunch of the popular boys—"

"Seventh AND eighth—"

"To write down what girls they like—"

"And then at the party we're gonna see if they match."

Lily felt like she was watching a Ping-Pong tournament. When her eyes stopped bouncing back and forth between them, she forced a smile.

"What if someone doesn't like anybody?" she said.

Both heads went back in laughter.

"Everybody likes somebody!" Ashley said.

"And don't worry," Chelsea said. "Nobody at the party'll tell anything."

"We'll swear to secrecy," Ashley said.

Lily nodded carefully, but the thoughts were tumbling over each other in her head.

The Girlz and I made that promise and nobody's ever broken it. But Ashley and Chelsea and their friends? Are they that loyal too?

Up until that moment, it would have been hard to believe. But looking at the two of them now, the way they smiled at Lily as if they'd been dying for years to invite her to one of their parties, she was tempted to trust them.

"So will you at least ask?" Chelsea said.

"And don't forget what I said about slamming your door," Ashley said. "Parents hate for you to shut them out. They'll do just about anything to make friends again."

"Okay," Lily said. "I'll get back to you."

"I should give you my number," Ashley said, and she stuck her hand into her backpack.

"But write down your boy-thing anyway," Chelsea said. "Just in case you do come."

"Here," Ashley said as she pushed her phone number across Lily's desk.

"Come over to my seat and get mine too," Chelsea said.

She grabbed Lily's wrist and pulled her out of the desk. "Cute shoes," she said as she almost hauled Lily across the room.

They're the same shoes I wear every day, Lily thought.

Chelsea sat down at her desk and pawed through the zipper compartment on her backpack while Lily stood beside her.

"You better squat down so Mrs. Stranglehold won't see you if the bell rings," Chelsea whispered.

Lily sank down and watched Chelsea scribble her phone number on a piece of stationery with some boy band's pictures on it.

"Which one do you like?" Chelsea asked.

Lily didn't know any of their names, so she pointed at one.

Chelsea blinked her large blue eyes at Lily. "That is so weird," she said. "That's the one I like too!"

"Wow," Lily said.

She was struggling for something else to add when the bell rang. Mrs. Reinhold closed the door. And there was Lily, out of her seat—again.

There was no way she was trying the crawl this time. Maybe she could just hurry around the back of the room while Mrs. Reinhold—Mrs. Stranglehold—was closing the door.

Snatching the phone number off of Chelsea's desk, Lily stuffed it into the pocket of her pants and headed for the back of the room.

Reni was in the desk behind Chelsea's, and she looked up at Lily, her eyes round.

She sees you, they said.

Lily sighed and turned around. As she did, she felt something poking at her hand, and she closed her fingers over a folded piece of paper. At the same moment, Mrs. Reinhold said, "That is your third tardy, Lilianna. Prepare your parents for my call."

Lily's "Is there a problem?" look failed her. She just nodded.

"Go to your seat," the teacher said. "Class—open your literature books to page thirty-five."

Somehow Lily got to her desk and dropped into it. In front of her, Ashley leaned back and without turning around, and almost without moving her mouth, she whispered, "I hope this doesn't mean you won't get to come."

Lily didn't dare answer her. She just propped open *Adventures in World Literature* and stared in humiliation at page thirty-five.

Almost before she could finish reading the assigned story, Mrs. Reinhold called for them to get out sheets of paper for a pop quiz. Lily could barely remember the answers to the five questions, and she was mortified when Mrs. Reinhold said for them to exchange papers.

Ashley whipped around, stuck her quiz on Lily's desk, and grabbed hers. When Lily turned it over, she saw some faint writing at the top in pencil, where in Mrs. Reinhold's class nothing was supposed to be written.

"Do you think you'll still get to come if she calls your mom?" the note said. "Erase this."

Lily was even more confused as she erased the note. Would she get to go anywhere for the next five years if Mrs. Reinhold called her mom? That was the question!

But Ashley had said parents hated to feel shut out. Maybe if she just talked to Mom and Dad about how unfair it all was. After all, today was the only time it had actually been her fault that she was late.

"Oh, yeah," Lily wrote lightly at the bottom of Ashley's paper.

This was one trick for passing notes she hadn't thought of. And speaking of notes—

Keeping her eyes warily on Mrs. Reinhold's back, she slid Reni's note out of her pocket and unfolded it inside her literature book.

It was a Lily-Gram: "Still spending the night tonight? 6:30 okay?"

Uh-oh, Lily thought. *BIG uh-oh.*

For once she was grateful for Mrs. Reinhold's watchful eyes. It gave her an excuse not to look over at Reni and give her an eye-answer.

What am I gonna do? Lily thought. She'd forgotten all about going to Reni's.

There was only one thing to do, of course, and she knew it. Reni had asked her first, so she would go to Reni's.

Besides, she reassured herself, *I don't "like" anybody, so now I don't have to worry about Ashley's game.*

She didn't want to risk passing Ashley a note, so she decided to wait until she could tell her face-to-face. Maybe between classes.

But when the bell rang and Mrs. Reinhold dismissed their row, she put a hand on Lily's shoulder as she came out of the aisle and said, "Let's chat for a moment, shall we?"

Lily looked in agony out the door. There were four people waiting for her—Reni, Suzy, Ashley, and Chelsea. She didn't know what was worse: having to sort all of them out or facing whatever Mrs. Reinhold had on her mind.

There was no choice, really. As soon as the last kid had filed out, Mrs. Reinhold closed the door and motioned for Lily to sit in the chair beside her desk.

"Next hour is my planning period," she said. "I'll write you a pass to your next class."

She sat in her own chair and folded her hands, with the spider-web veins on them, primly on the desktop. By now, Lily couldn't swallow. She did manage, however, to speak.

"I wish you wouldn't call my parents," she said. "Today I was where I shouldn't have been, but the other two times—"

"You've hit the nail right on the head," Mrs. Reinhold said. "You were certainly not where you should be today."

"You're right," Lily agreed, although she wasn't sure exactly what Mrs. Reinhold was talking about.

"I generally don't meddle in the social affairs of my students," she said, "but I just want to alert you that if you want to stay out of trouble, you will stick with the friends you currently have. Reni and Suzanne are excellent choices."

"They're two of my best friends!" Lily said.

"Now, mind you, I am not casting aspersions on Ashley and Chelsea. They're both bright girls with a great deal of potential. But at the moment they do not have their priorities straight, and I fear that's going to land them in hot water. I would hate to see you end up there as well, when you are off to such a good start in middle school." She indicated a change in subject by adjusting her glasses. "Mr. Miniver says you're doing beautifully on the newspaper staff. He's never seen such performance out of a seventh grader. You are in fact the only one he took on this first semester, and he's hoping to find more like you after Christmas." The wrinkles at the corners of her eyes twitched. "I told him he will never find anyone exactly like you. I hope you won't prove me wrong by trying to become like everyone else."

Before Lily could answer—though she had no idea what she would have said—Mrs. Reinhold pushed her chair back from her desk and stood up.

"I've probably said more than I should have already, Lilianna," she said. "I trust you know that not a word of this leaves this room."

Lily didn't know whether to shake her head or nod, so she said, "You can trust me."

"I hope so. Now let me write you that pass. Who's your fourth-period teacher?"

"Ms. Ferringer," Lily said. Her head felt as if it would spin right off. What was going on? One minute she was flattered that two girls who had always made fun of her at every possible opportunity were suddenly all over her. The next minute, Mrs. Reinhold was telling her she shouldn't go near them. And then there was Reni. And Suzy—

Of course, if Mrs. Reinhold called her house, none of it would matter anyway because Lily was going to be in solitary confinement.

"Mrs. Reinhold?" she said.

"I'm the only one in the room."

"What time were you planning to call my mother?"

"Why?"

"Um—"

"I don't understand 'um.' Think about what you want to say and then talk."

That was just it. If she thought about it for too long, she'd have to face the fact that she was about to tell a lie.

"Well?" Mrs. Reinhold said.

"I just want to know because my mom doesn't get home until after 6:30."

There. It was out. She resisted the urge to reach up and see if her nose was growing. As it was, she couldn't meet Mrs. Reinhold's gaze.

"I thought your mother was a teacher at the high school."

"She is."

"I suppose sports practices and games keep her out until all hours."

"That's right!" Lily wished she'd thought of that one herself.

"It's 6:30 then." Mrs. Reinhold held out the pass to her. "She's going to be disappointed in you, isn't she?"

Lily nodded. The lump was forming in her throat again.

"I would like to skip it, I truly would, but I can't start making exceptions. As it is, I'm one of the few teachers left here who holds students accountable for their mistakes. If I fudge, you children are lost."

"I understand," Lily said. That was the second lie of the morning.

With the pass in hand, she hurried on to Ms. Ferringer's class. Fortunately, the lecture was already under way. Lily was able to slide into her seat and avoid everybody's eyes.

But she couldn't avoid the Lily-Grams. Two of them appeared on her desk while she sharpened her pencil, making her wish she'd never invented them.

"So can we talk after school?" Suzy's said.

Lily answered: "Call my house at 6:00 tonight. We'll talk then."

Reni's said: "Tonight? Okay?"

Lily gnawed off a whole eraser before writing: "Yes. Can it be 6:00 instead?"

She couldn't avoid the accusing voice in her head that said, *You're just making sure you're gone before Mrs. Reinhold calls!*

But that was okay. Mrs. Reinhold had already said she didn't really want to call Lily's mom. She herself knew two of those tardies hadn't actually been Lily's fault. And Mom and Dad could ground her on Saturday night, when she didn't have anything planned.

Once the Lily-Grams were delivered, Lily felt a little more like things were settled. Her heart was lighter as she hurried to the staff room for lunch. Then it dropped like a bundle of wet newspapers—right to her toes.

Lance was the only one there, and when Lily came in, he looked up at her and smiled—that's right, smiled. And his blue eyes sparkled like a glass of 7-Up.

"Hey, Lil!" he said. "So, I hear you and my sister are pretty tight. You're coming over tonight—right?"

Only when Lance motioned her over with his head did Lily realize she'd been staring at him for a full thirty seconds and that her mouth was probably gaping open.

She started to move toward him, and he said, "Close the door."

She did. When she turned around, he had a chair ready for her.

"Okay, here's the thing," he said when she'd sunk stiffly into it. "All of us on the staff made this pact at the beginning of the year that we weren't gonna let any seventh graders on the staff until second semester. Mr. Miniver doesn't know about it, which doesn't really matter because the other seventh graders we got in here before you were all losers."

"Oh," Lily said.

"The day after your column first came out, everybody else wanted to vote you in right away, but I said no." Lance shrugged casually. "No offense, but just because you could write that good didn't mean you were automatically cool. So anyway, yesterday my sister and her friend—what's her name?"

"Chelsea?" Lily said.

"Yeah—they're two of, like, about five cool kids in the whole seventh grade. I'm talkin' to them and I ask them about you, and they just, like, look at each other—"

Eyes rolling and lips curling, Lily thought.

"And they're all, 'We're gonna invite her to our sleepover tomorrow night.' So—I figure you're okay. We're gonna vote you in at lunch. Which means you might, like, not want to be here."

"Oh, sure!" Lily said. *I think I'll go hide in the bathroom!*

Lance was still smiling at her, blue eyes sizzling, as she got up.

"So—does anybody ever get voted off the staff?" she asked.

Lance slanted his eyes toward the door and lowered his voice. "Mr. Miniver doesn't know this either, but we would vote somebody off if it turned out they weren't cool anymore." He snickered. "But once you're cool, you're always cool, unless you really mess up."

"But if Mr. Miniver doesn't know about it, how can you—"

"We'd just make life so miserable for the person, they'd drop out on their own. Don't worry about it—when Ashley says somebody's, like, 'so sweet"—his voice went up into a soprano—"that's like—you're in. Dude, I wouldn't even admit she was my sister if she wasn't cool."

"I so know what you mean," Lily muttered. And then she did head for the bathroom.

It was the longest afternoon in the history of middle school, Lily was sure of that. Every minute was like an hour as she chewed on what she was supposed to do, and when she got home, she was no closer to an answer.

"If I go to Reni's at six," she told Otto, "I won't have to worry about being grounded tonight. But that means I don't go to Ashley's, and if I don't go to Ashley's, I'm not cool and then the staff'll make my life miserable—whatever that means—and I won't get to be Answer Girl anymore!"

Otto jumped down from the bed as if he had the perfect solution and came back with a slimy, defurred tennis ball, which he dropped into her lap.

"That is so not helping," she said.

Nor did it help when she got out her journal and tried to figure it out there. None of her lists of pros and cons or writing out her frustrations did anything but give her an ink stain on her middle finger.

And the worst contribution yet came when Dad brought her the phone. "I think it's Reni," he said. "Don't talk too long now, because I need to make some calls."

After Lily said hi, Reni launched right in. "So—are you coming over tonight or not?"

Lily stalled. "Didn't I say I would in my note?"

"Yeah—but then I rode the late bus home after school, and I thought I heard that girl Bernadette, or whatever her name is, say she was going to a sleepover at Ashley Adamson's, and that you were gonna be there."

"Why would Ashley invite me?" Lily said. Her heart was slamming against the walls of her chest.

"Why don't you tell me? You were pretty tight with her and Chelsea third period today."

Lily couldn't tell her. All she could do was try to swallow the lump in her throat.

"By the way," Reni said, "what did Mrs. Reinhold do to you?"

"She's gonna call my parents at—"

Lily stopped. An idea was sneaking around in the dark places at the edges of her brain.

No—that would be so not a good thing to do! her conscience cried out.

But Lily opened her mouth, and it came out. "She's gonna call my parents this afternoon, and I'll probably get grounded and won't be able to come over. We probably shouldn't plan on it."

"They won't ground you!"

"Yes, they will."

"How do you know? You never get in trouble." There was a sudden pause. "What were you doing over at Chelsea's desk anyway?"

She was giving me her phone number, and Reni, I don't know what to do about this. I'm so mixed up—you gotta help me!

That, Lily knew, was what she should have said—what she really wanted to say.

Instead, she said, "I have to go. My dad needs to use the phone."

As Lily hung up, she felt like it was the first true thing that had come out of her mouth all day. She took the phone downstairs and tapped on the door to her dad's study.

"That you, Lilliputian?" he said.

He sounded so warm, so kind—it made Lily feel like she was about to cry. She swallowed down the lump and pushed open the door. If she didn't do this quick, she was going to lose her nerve and then she'd still be in the same miserable spot.

She took a deep breath. "Here's the phone, Dad—do you care if I go to Ashley Adamson's house for a sleepover—Mom knows her mom 'cause we've gone to school together since first grade—I have to leave before 6:30, so could Art take me to her house?"

Dad took off his glasses. "Can we breathe now?"

"Yeah," Lily said, though she wasn't sure she could.

"On one condition," he said.

"What?"

"You and I spend some time together tomorrow. Go to Friendly's for an ice cream. Rummage through the bookstore together. Can you pencil me in?"

At that point, the tears did come, and Lily smacked at them with the backs of her hands. Dad looked bewildered.

"I didn't mean to make you cry," he said. "Was it something I said?"

Yes! Lily wanted to wail. *You're too nice to me, and I don't deserve it!*

But she said, "No. I just—why does everything change, Dad? Oh—never mind!" And she turned on her heel and escaped to her room.

She stayed there, even when she heard Mom come in downstairs with Joe. She watched the clock until it was ten minutes to six, and then, sleeping bag under her arm, she went up to Art's room. He was shaking saliva out of this saxophone mouthpiece.

"Did Dad ask you to take me to Ashley's?" she said.

"No—but I will. I gotta go out anyway. Where does she live?"

"Over on Summer Avenue."

"Since when did you start hangin' out with rich kids?" Art asked. He stuffed his wallet into the back pocket of his jeans and grabbed his car keys. "I thought you were little Miss Bleeding Heart."

"What does that mean?" Lily said.

"It means you're always for the underdogs—the Dooleys of the human world."

"My friends aren't dogs!" Lily said.

"Yeah, but they all got problems," he said, following her down the stairs. "One of 'em's kinda blimpy. One of 'em barely speaks English. One of 'em barely speaks at all. Hey, did I tell you that same girl called for you last night and hung up before I could get her name?"

Lily shook her head. She was barely listening to him. Her focus was on getting out the front door before Mrs. Reinhold called.

She waited until she was about to close the door behind her before she yelled, "Bye, Mom!"

"Where are you going?" Mom shouted back.

"Dad knows—he said I could. Bye!"

Then she closed the door, a little harder than she meant to, and sprinted toward Art's Subaru. She heard the phone ringing behind her, and she was pretty sure that was the only reason Mom didn't run after her for more details. Lily was barely in the car before she was saying, "Okay—let's go. I'm gonna be late."

Art was more than happy to gun the motor and take off. Lily didn't dare look back.

When they got to Ashley's, Lily was surprised to find that there were only three girls there besides her: Ashley, Chelsea, and Bernadette. Somehow she'd expected Ashley's entire entourage.

Bernadette was one of those girls who always looked as if she'd just combed her hair, freshened up her lip gloss, and ironed her outfit. She was new at Cedar Hills, but Ashley and Chelsea had absorbed her into their group almost the first day. She was clearly the prettiest girl in the seventh grade, and the Girlz had figured Ashley wanted to befriend her before she became competition.

Bernadette was now perched on a mauve window-seat cushion in Ashley's room, feet crossed daintily in a pair of socks with a DKNY logo on the heel. Her perfect curls were caught up in one of those clips Art always said reminded him of some kind of medieval torture tool. Looking around at her, Ashley, and Chelsea, who were all similarly dressed, Lily felt a little tortured. She was wearing sweats and Nikes that she was sure no amount of the right attitude could cover up.

But Bernadette patted the window-seat cushion and said, "Sit by me, Lily."

Lily dropped her sleeping bag and ventured over. She looked around for the snacks that were always a huge part of any sleepover from the time you arrived until you stumbled sleepily home the next morning. Maybe if she had something to do with her hands, she wouldn't feel klutzy.

There wasn't a chip in sight—not even so much as a stray can of soda. Feeling like an octopus, Lily sat on two of her eight hands on the cushion and looked around Ashley's mauve and maroon room. It looked like it had been picked up out of an expensive furniture store showroom and transplanted here.

"Where's your paper?" Chelsea said.

"Huh?" Lily said.

Bernadette rubbed her toe lightly against Lily's leg. "Your paper with who you like on it. Did you bring it?"

Lily wondered if the window seat doubled as a storage cabinet. She'd like to climb right into it.

"Here," Ashley said. She stuck out a green gel pen and a pad of paper with "From Ashley's Desk" printed on each piece.

"That's neat stationery," Lily said. "Where'd you get it?" Maybe if she stalled long enough, Ashley would forget about this game.

"I don't know," Ashley said. "Some relative sent it to me last Christmas. Like I ever sit at a desk if I don't have to!"

"Duh," and "I hear you," Chelsea and Bernadette echoed.

"Yeah," Lily said. Actually she'd been thinking that it would be fun to print up some Lily-Grams and give each of the Girlz a set for Christmas. The thought gnawed at her until it sunk its teeth in.

"You're gonna want some privacy," Bernadette said.

"We'll go get the food," Ashley said.

They headed for the door while Lily stared at the pad, her mind completely empty of any boys' names. It was even hard to remember her brothers' names with Chelsea hovering at her elbow. Acting tough in school was one thing. Pulling it off with all three of them staring at her was another.

"Come on, Chels," Ashley said. Then she flashed Lily a brilliant smile. "I'm so glad you came," she said.

As the door closed behind the three of them, Lily wasn't so sure she was glad. She looked miserably at the blank pad. The entire party seemed to be centered on the who-likes-who game, and so far that wasn't exactly a blast. An ache formed in her chest as she thought about being at Reni's right now, eating her mom's brownies and howling over old sitcoms on Nickelodeon.

But she got an even bigger ache when she remembered what Lance had said—about Ashley and Chelsea saying Lily was cool. About that being the deciding factor in her being kept on the newspaper staff—

The green gel pen jerked in Lily's hand. That was it, of course—the way to keep Ashley and Chelsea and now Bernadette thinking she was cool enough. With the three girls' footsteps already on the stairs, Lily quickly wrote Lance Adamson on the paper and folded it up, just as the door opened.

"Did you do it?" Chelsea said as she burst in and tossed a bag of Doritos toward Ashley's white wicker rocking chair. She was back at Lily's elbow practically before it landed.

"Yeah," Lily said. "Where do you want me to put it?"

Chelsea poked out a hand. "Right here."

"God, Chelsea," Ashley said.

Lily felt herself flinch. She couldn't imagine any of the Girlz using God's name that way.

Of course, I haven't used his name at all lately, she thought.

Right now definitely didn't seem like the time. Even thinking about God made her face go blotchy.

By this time, Ashley had taken Lily's paper and dropped it into a basket with hearts painted on it. The corners of several other pieces poked up out of it.

"That's everybody," she said.

"Can we start?" Chelsea said.

For the first time since she'd arrived, Lily really looked at her. She'd never seen Chelsea flushed in the cheeks the way she was now, as if she were up to the $500,000 question on *Who Wants to Be a Millionaire*. She was actually chewing on her glitter-polished fingernails.

"Would you chill?" Ashley said to her.

"Here, Lily," Bernadette said. "I brought you a Coke."

Lily took the can, which was warm, and continued to watch Chelsea. She had never seen anybody so freaked out over a game—especially one that seemed to have absolutely no point.

Bernadette retrieved the chip bag and squeezed onto the window seat with Chelsea and Lily. Ashley sat on the floor facing them, holding the basket. Lily was sure that if she didn't open one of those pieces of paper soon, Chelsea was going to throw herself out the window.

"Do Lily's first!" Chelsea said.

"No—I'm just gonna pick whichever one my hand touches," Ashley said. "And it is—"

She peered at the half sheet of binder paper that had been ripped out of somebody's notebook. "Leo. He likes Chelsea."

Lily expected a squeal. Instead, Chelsea pretended to vomit over the side of the seat.

"Isn't he one of Shad's friends?" Bernadette said, twirling a curl.

"Yes," Ashley said.

"He's cute! Why don't you like him?"

"He's so immature!" Chelsea said. "Pick another one."

Ashley was already reading. She tossed the paper toward them with a smile. "It's Shad's. He says he likes me."

"Duh," Bernadette said. "You're only, like, together."

Lily looked over Bernadette's shoulder at the paper. It sure didn't look like Shad's handwriting. You could actually read it.

"Go on," Chelsea said, waving her hand at Ashley.

"Bernadette likes—" Ashley looked up wickedly. "I didn't know this."

"You do now."

"Tell me," Chelsea said—her face now magenta.

We're gonna need the paramedics in a minute, Lily thought.

"Doug," Ashley said.

"Doug on the newspaper staff?" Lily said.

Bernadette smiled. "He's like a big teddy bear."

"Sorry," Ashley said, "but I didn't ask him to do one. I would have if I'd known—"

"That's okay," Bernadette said. "I already know he likes me too."

Lily stared at her. How in the world would you know something like that? She squirmed uncomfortably on the cushion. These girls couldn't be any more different from Lily and the Girlz if they'd been chimpanzees. Why had they invited her here?

"Hurry up," Chelsea was saying.

"Ashley likes Shad," Ashley read.

"Duh. Do another one."

"Daniel—likes Bernadette."

"Is that Shad's other friend?" Bernadette said.

"Yeah," Lily said. *He's an absurd little creep just like the other two.*

"Okay—Chelsea likes—"

"No! Don't do mine yet!"

Chelsea was screaming like the house was on fire, but Ashley just looked at her calmly.

"It's the way you play the game," she said.

As far as Lily could see, Ashley was making up the rules as she went along, but she wasn't changing them for Chelsea.

"Chelsea likes Lance," she read.

Lily went cold. She was glad she hadn't taken a drink of the Coke or she'd have spit it all over Ashley.

"Lance—Adamson?" Lily said. "I mean—your brother?"

"Do you know any other Lances?" Chelsea said. She looked as if she sincerely hoped so, and with everything she had, Lily wished she hadn't put a last name down.

"Can I change mine?" Lily said.

"No, that's against the rules," Ashley said.

"Why—did you just stop liking one guy and start liking somebody else in the last two minutes?" Bernadette said.

Lily shook her head. "I just put the wrong name down."

By now, Ashley and Chelsea were having an eye-conversation, and anybody could have broken that code.

I told you, Ashley was saying.

Nuh-uh, Chelsea was saying back.

"So—there's two left," Bernadette said. "Read them."

Ashley pried her eyes away from Chelsea long enough to look at the next piece of folded paper she picked up. It was obviously Lily's.

Please, God, Lily thought, *please make her have dyslexia—just for a minute!*

"Lily," Ashley said, "likes Lance Adamson."

"Oops," Bernadette said.

"But he doesn't like me!" Lily said. "I mean—he likes me—but not like that—he just likes me on the newspaper—and I only put his name down because—"

She couldn't finish—not with Chelsea shooting a round of ammunition at her with her eyes.

"You like him," Bernadette said, nodding sagely. "Or else your face wouldn't be so red."

"No!" Lily said. "My face is just red because—" *I'm about to die.*

"Well, there's only one way to solve this," Bernadette said. She nodded toward the basket. "See who Lance likes."

Lily felt relief pulsing through her. Of course! Lance would have written Chelsea's name—if he could remember it—or even KJ's or Crystal's—and that would wipe the I'm-going-to-kill-you-Lily-Robbins look off of Chelsea's face. *I'll even pretend I'm heartbroken,* Lily thought.

"Let me read it," Chelsea said, snatching the paper out of Ashley's hand. In spite of her protests, Chelsea fumbled the note open and stared. Whatever Lance had written, it wasn't what Chelsea wanted to see, that was clear. Her eyes went down into murderous slits.

"Could I have it back now?" Ashley said in an icy voice.

Chelsea thrust it at her. As Ashley read, her face went blank.

"What does it say?" Bernadette said, abandoning the chip bag and reaching for the paper.

Ashley drew it away, looked at it again, and then narrowed her own eyes.

"I'm gonna kill my brother," she said.

No, kill me first! Lily wanted to shriek. *Put me out of my misery!*

"What did he write?" Bernadette said. "I'm dying here!"

Ashley looked at Chelsea. "It says he likes the Answer Girl."

He is so gonna get it from me," Ashley said. "I told him to write a name."

"Who is the Answer Girl, anyway?" Bernadette said.

"Nobody knows but the newspaper staff—"

Ashley stopped, and suddenly the three of them looked as if they'd been given a silent cue. They all turned their heads toward Lily at the same time and looked at her with the same question in their eyes. Bernadette voiced it.

"You're on the staff, Lily. Who is it?"

Lily had been scrambling for an answer long before they'd asked her. She forced a laugh.

"Do you think they're gonna tell me, a seventh grader?"

"No," Ashley said. She shoved her hair behind her ears like she was getting down to business. "But they think you're at least semi-cool or you wouldn't still be on the staff."

"They just voted me on officially today, though," Lily said. "And I haven't been to the staff room since then—"

"But they'll tell you now," Chelsea said, bobbing her head up and down as if that alone would make it happen. "I betcha if you asked Lance right now, he'd tell you."

She actually went for the door, but Ashley said, "He's out. You don't really think he'd stay home on a Friday night, do you?"

"Duh," Bernadette said.

"But you could find out Monday," Chelsea said to Lily as she sat down next to Ashley. She gave a wicked cackle. "Then I'll know who to kill."

"You so could," Ashley said.

Bernadette nudged Lily with her elbow. "You want to find out too, don't you? Since you like him?"

Lily was shaking her head before she even knew what she was going to say. "I don't really like him that much—I mean, no offense, I know he's your brother and all that, Ashley—but there's somebody else I like more."

Chelsea's eyes turned into slits. "Then why didn't you write his name down?"

"Because," Lily said, "you don't know him." *How could you? I don't even know him!*

Chelsea threw back her head and gave the most genuine laugh Lily had ever heard from her. Ashley cupped her hands around Chelsea's ear and whispered in it. Bernadette looked seriously at Lily.

"I'm really glad," she said. "I hate it when guys break up a friendship."

"Oh, yeah," Chelsea said. "I was just starting to like you. If you'd really liked Lance, I'd have had to start hating you again."

"One thing, though," Ashley said. "You have to promise not to tell anybody what went on in here tonight."

"Especially not Reni and all of them," Chelsea put in.

Why would I tell Reni what a liar I am? Lily thought. She nodded and raised her hand, courtroom style.

"Okay," Bernadette said, swinging the chip bag in Lily's direction. "Tell us about this guy you like."

"Yeah," Ashley said. "How come we don't know him? I thought we knew, like, all the cool kids."

"He isn't a geek, is he?" Chelsea said.

"Uh, no," Bernadette said. She patted Lily's knee. "The Lil-meister wouldn't like somebody geeky. She's cool."

"That's totally true," Ashley said. "So tell us."

For a second, nothing would come out of Lily's mouth. All she could think about was Reni saying, *What were you doing over there anyway?* And her dad saying, *We expected more out of you, Lilliputian*, and her mom saying, *So, basically you're turning into a liar. Is that what's happening here, Lil?* She could even hear Art saying, *You're as much of a moron as I used to think you were.* Yikes, Otto would probably even start sleeping in Joe's room or something—

But she did open her mouth, and with Ashley, Chelsea, and Bernadette hanging on each word, she said, "He doesn't go to our school. He's not even from around here."

They all looked disappointed. Lily stuffed a chip into her mouth. When somebody knocked on the door, she almost melted into a puddle of momentary relief.

There wasn't much melting time, however. It was Ashley's mother, and she poked her carefully styled head into the room and said, "Lily? Your parents are here to get you."

"No, Mom," Ashley said in an annoyed voice. "Tell them she's spending the night."

"I did," Mrs. Adamson said, "but apparently they weren't completely clear on that when Lily left the house. I'm sure you can work it out with them, Sweetie."

Lily was sure she couldn't—not in a hundred thousand years. Knowing her face was turning crimson, she picked up her sleeping bag.

"No!" Ashley said. "Make them let you stay!"

"Parents," Bernadette said, with Mrs. Adamson still within hearing range. "Don't you hate them sometimes?"

"Uh, try all the time," Chelsea said.

Then as one, they rolled their eyes.

"You want me to come talk to them?" Ashley said.

"No," Lily said. "They're pretty stubborn." And obviously pretty mad or they wouldn't have come over here to haul her away. Her heart was pounding so hard it hurt.

"So sneak out and come back after they go to bed," Chelsea said.

"Yeah," Ashley said. "Throw some of those pebbles from our fountain at my window, and we'll come down and let you in."

"Do it," Bernadette said.

"Sure," Lily said.

But the vision she had in her mind was not of climbing down the rose trellis. It was of her parents, waiting at the bottom of the Adamsons' stairs with disappointment and anger taking turns on their faces.

The minute she got to the landing, she saw that she was correct, right down to the way Mom's arms were folded. By the time she reached them, Lily could barely breathe.

"Sorry again to disturb you," Dad said to Mrs. Adamson.

"It's not a problem," she said. "I know how it is with girls at this age." She cheerfully patted Lily's back. "Please come back again, Lily. I know how much Ashley likes you."

"Ashley likes you?" Mom said when the front door had closed behind them and they were nearing the end of the driveway. "All I hear from you is how mean she is. What is going on, Lil?"

"Dad said I could come," Lily said as she slid miserably into the van. If she'd dared, she would have gone for the very back seat. But the way Mom's eyes were flashing, she thought she better not.

"I know that," Mom said. She slammed the passenger door and twisted around in the seat. Dad started the motor. "But we both smell manipulation."

"What's that?" Lily said. She knew—but maybe a long definition from Dad would buy some time.

"It means you very carefully arranged to be out of the house when Mrs. Reinhold called—and without leaving a phone number or address. Your father couldn't even remember whose house you'd gone to, and frankly, Lilianna, I think you were counting on that."

Mom was calling her Lilianna. Not good. She was obviously in huge trouble. A lump the size of Ashley's whole house was forming in her throat.

"Did Art tell on me?" she managed to say.

"Under duress," Mom said. "When he called in to tell us where he was going next and I asked where he'd taken you, he tried to pretend we had a bad connection." She twitched an eyebrow. "Only when I threatened to take away his driver's license did he spill it."

Lily couldn't blame him for that. She couldn't blame anybody—except herself. But it was all such a tangled mess. What else could she have done?

"Why are you crying?" Mom said.

Lily hadn't even realized she was. She smeared the tears on her cheeks with her fingers. "I don't know," she said.

"There's a lot of that going on today, Lilliputian," Dad said. "You want to tell us what's up?"

Dad's eyes were soft in the rearview mirror, and even Mom wasn't staring at her quite so hard. Still, all Lily could think to say was, "I'm just stupid, that's all."

"You are far from stupid," Dad said, "which is why we're mystified by this behavior. I think you're just not considering what you're doing very carefully."

"Considering it?" Mom said. "I don't think it's going through your brain at all! If it were, you'd see that you are abusing our trust, taking up with girls you've despised, and rightfully so, since the first grade, and neglecting friendships you've been nurturing for a long time."

"I'm not neglecting the Girlz!" Lily said.

"Then why did you tell Suzy you'd be home to talk to her on the phone and then hightail it out of there before she could call?"

The lump got bigger. Lily could barely see her hands in her lap for the tears.

"And then there was Mrs. Reinhold's phone call," Mom said. "At 6:30 on the dot, the time she said you told her I got home. Since when was I not home by 5:00?"

"You're always home by five," Lily mumbled.

"So am I correct that you told her 6:30 so you could be gone when she called?"

Lily nodded.

"Answer your mother," Dad said.

So much for softness. It may have been the sharpest Lily had ever heard his voice directed at her. It cut through her like a hatchet.

"Yes," Lily struggled to say. "I did it on purpose."

"Why?" Mom said. "Are we such monsters that you thought we were going to hang you up by your thumbs or something?"

"I thought you wouldn't let me go to Ashley's, and I had to go—"

Lily stopped there. She couldn't tell her mom and dad how stupid she really was—not when she was already looking pretty bad in that category.

"Why didn't you tell Ashley the same thing you told Reni?" Mom said.

Lily's mouth fell open. "Reni?" she said.

"When Reni called to try to convince us to let you come to her house tonight and start your 'groundation' tomorrow, she was more than a little surprised to find out that you'd gone to Ashley's."

"I don't know how you're keeping all these lies straight," Dad said. "I'm completely confused myself."

He did look bewildered—and disappointed—and angry—all the things she had never wanted to see on his face. Mom was all of that times ten. Lily was sobbing.

"You spoke the truth on one count, though," Mom said, obviously unmoved by Lily's tears. "You thought we'd ground you when Mrs. Reinhold told us about your tardies—and that is exactly what we're going to do. Did you forget that I'm a high school teacher, Lil? I know you have plenty of time to get from one class to another."

"I didn't forget," Lily said—in a voice that was barely audible.

"I have a tendency to be late now and then myself," Dad said. "I'm more concerned about the lies."

"And Mrs. Reinhold is more concerned about this little shift in your choice of friends. She confirmed what you've known all along—Ashley and Chelsea and the people they hang out with are shallow and self-serving. For them to suddenly want to be your bosom buddies means there is something in it for them."

"Is there something in it for you, Lilliputian?" Dad asked.

They were back in their own driveway now, and Lily wanted to run for the house and lock herself up in her room until she was too old and wise to make stupid mistakes anymore. As it was, all she could do was cry.

"I think that's enough for tonight," Dad said.

"Go on up to your room," Mom said. "We'll talk about this in the morning."

Lily was more than glad to go. When she got there, she didn't even pour her heart out to Otto and China. She just dug her head into her pillow and sobbed until she fell asleep.

Otto woke Lily the next morning, whining to go out. Dad was in the kitchen when she went down to open the back door. Lily could barely look at him. In fact, she tried to slip into the dining room before he looked up from his newspaper, but without even moving it, he said, "Get dressed. You and I are going out."

"I thought I was grounded," Lily said.

"You're grounded from doing anything with your friends until you get yourself sorted out." He looked at her over the top of the *Times*. "I'm assuming I'm not considered a friend at this point, so this is different."

"We're friends," Lily said. Her chest was aching.

"Are we?" Dad said, folding the paper as he talked. "I thought friends were honest with each other. Trusted each other. Shared their issues."

Lily couldn't say anything.

"Go get dressed," Dad said. "Let's see if we can remedy that."

"Where's Mom? Does she know?"

Dad's eyes smiled. "At least we're making some progress. She took Joe to soccer and then she's going grocery shopping. And yes, she knows."

As she trailed upstairs and pulled some jeans out of her closet, Lily wished she could turn the clock back to yesterday when Dad had asked her to save some time for him today. She wished she had sat down right then and there and told him everything. Maybe then, she wouldn't have ditched Reni and flaked out on Suzy. She'd be going out to do something fun today.

What about Ashley, Chelsea, and Bernadette? she thought. Could Dad have helped me solve that? If she hadn't gone, they'd have told Lance she was a loser, and he and the staff would make life miserable for her. They might even make her give up Answer Girl.

And that was the only thing that made her special. Everybody else seemed to have that certain "thing" except her. Reni had her violin. Kresha was astonishing everybody with the way she was learning English. Even Zooey was getting attention for losing weight and developing a figure that was better than any of theirs.

Who am I if I'm not Answer Girl? she thought. And I might not even be that for much longer—not if Ashley and the others find out Lance likes me. And not if they tell him I'm not cool because I didn't sneak out and go back to Ashley's last night.

Suddenly she didn't want to go out with Dad at all. She wanted to get back in bed and pull the covers over her head.

But she pulled on her jeans and a T-shirt and met him at the front door.

"How about the mall?" he said.

"Sure."

It didn't occur to her until they were almost there that Dad usually hated the mall. He preferred dusty old used bookstores and antique shops and coffee shops where smart people hung out. Usually they went to places like Moorestown together, where there were plenty of those things for them to enjoy together. Obviously "enjoying" wasn't his purpose.

When they got there, they began strolling past stores as if they did it every weekend. For what seemed to Lily like eternity itself, they walked along without talking. Finally, when she was close to tears again, Dad said, "How about breakfast at McDonald's? You haven't eaten yet."

"Okay," Lily said, though she wasn't sure she could gag down so much as an Egg McMuffin.

When they were settled at a corner table with two orders of pancakes and sausage, Dad still didn't say much beyond, "How are you supposed to get the syrup out of these little things?" Finally, Lily couldn't stand it any longer.

"I'm sorry about last night," she said. "You guys can ground me for a whole month—two months—and I won't complain. I know I was wrong, and you should punish me—for as long as you think."

"I already told you how long you're grounded for," Dad said.

"You did?"

"Yes. I said you're grounded from doing things with your friends until you get sorted out. However long that takes is up to you."

"That'll be 'til I graduate, then," Lily said. She set down her plastic fork.

"It's that bad, is it?"

"Yes. If I tell everybody the truth, I'm not gonna have any friends—period."

"I don't know. Since you said that, I'm starting to feel friendlier already."

"But you're my father! You have to be my friend!"

"I don't think friendship is in my job description as a father," Dad said. "I'm supposed to be your adviser, your guide, your provider, your disciplinarian, your guardian, your spiritual director—but not necessarily your friend. That part depends on you."

"And all that trust and stuff you were talking about before," Lily said.

"Is that so hard?"

"Yes."

"Why?"

Lily stared down at her now lukewarm pancakes.

"There are obviously things you're having a hard time telling me," Dad said. "Girl things, I assume?"

Lily nodded.

He chuckled. "Then don't even try! Let me just tell you this: no matter what it is that has you so confused, you know you can go to God with it. He's the father who wrote the job description for the rest of us."

"I forget to," Lily said.

"There's your trouble."

"I'd probably remember more if he'd answer—but I don't hear anything. He's not like you—or the Answer Girl."

Dad looked puzzled. "Who's the Answer Girl?"

Lily glanced cautiously around the McDonald's dining room, and then leaned forward. Dad leaned too.

"This is a secret," she said. "You can only tell Mom, okay? Not even Art or Joe."

Dad nodded solemnly, and because there wasn't a trace of a smile in his eyes, Lily told him about the advice column, how successful it was, how people said Answer Girl was a genius. When she was finished, he nodded thoughtfully.

"Impressive," he said. "Where do you get your answers to write down?"

"Once I got one from Art—"

"That's a little frightening."

"—but mostly I just think about what I would do in that situation, and that's what I write."

"So it's like a little voice inside your head."

"I guess so, yeah."

Dad ate a few more bites of pancake before he said, "Maybe Answer Girl ought to be listening to her own advice—really listening."

"Sometimes there isn't time, though! Stuff happens so fast, I can't even think!"

"Then make time. There are very few situations that couldn't benefit from waiting until you are really sure what to do, until you have listened to that little voice. Unless you have a gun held to your head or something like that, I suggest you try it."

"But what do I say to my friends? 'Hold on while I try to hear this little voice in my head?' They'd think I was Looney Tunes!"

"You can say, 'I'll get back to you on that,' or 'Let me give that some thought,' or—'I have to go to the bathroom.'"

"Go to the bathroom!"

Dad grinned. "It'll buy you some time. I've used it."

"Nuh-uh!"

"I used it just last night when your mother was all ready to drag you out of what's-her-name's house by the hair. I said, 'Just a minute—I need to use the restroom.' Then I sat in there and thought about it—"

"That's okay, Dad," Lily said. "I get the idea."

Dad was quiet while they finished breakfast and then strolled out into the mall again. There was plenty of time to think, but Lily didn't hear any little voices. She did pray, though.

God, I'm sorry I've been stupid and haven't been coming to you. But I need to hear you once in a while, okay? Please talk to me.

She was going to go on, but her eyes snagged on movement a few stores ahead of them. Two girls bolted out of Claire's, laughing loud enough to be heard over the crowd of early shoppers. Even Dad noticed them.

"Those two are up to no good," he said. "Anybody you know?"

Lily was about to shake her head when she realized one of the girls was Marcie McCleary. The other one she didn't recognize until they were closer. It was Heidi Hinson—the closest thing to a gang chick Lily had ever known.

What's Marcie doing with her? Lily wondered. *I thought she was all into Ashley and—*

Then something familiar nagged in a corner of her brain.

Marcie had said something about finding a friend who wanted to be with her—because Lily had told her to.

But I didn't tell her to take up with that kind of girl! Lily thought.

"I could be wrong," Dad said, "but I think those two just did a little shoplifting."

Lily watched Marcie and Heidi hurry through the people, their laughter still audible long after they had disappeared from view.

"Are you gonna do something?" Lily said.

Dad took off his glasses and chewed on the earpiece. "I'll have to get back to you on that, Lilliputian," he said. "Right now, I'm going to visit the restroom."

Lily sat down on a bench to wait for him. Two seconds hadn't gone by when she spotted three boys in front of the pet store across from her, banging on the windows and freaking out the guinea pigs. It didn't take another two seconds to realize it was Shad and his accomplices, Leo and Daniel.

Does every low life at Cedar Hills Middle School hang out at the mall on Saturdays? Lily thought.

No sooner had she thought it than another figure appeared on the pet shop scene, a female one. She hurried up behind Shad and put her hands over his eyes. It was Ashley.

Lily came up off the bench and looked for a place to hide, her mind bouncing off the walls inside her head. *If she sees me she'll ask me why I didn't come back last night—She'll really think I'm a geek when she finds out I'm at the mall with my dad—And she hangs out with somebody that thinks scaring little furry animals is funny—*

The thoughts were coming so fast she couldn't grab on to any of them. And none of them was coming in a little voice that made sense. Dad had said to wait until that voice told her what to do.

Lily headed for the bathroom.

She was no clearer when she came out, but at least Ashley, Shad, and the others were gone. Dad had had better luck. They went into Claire's, and Dad advised the manager to check her stock carefully and watch for two girls in too-big jeans with their navels showing. Although the manager said that described just about every customer she had, she thanked him and hurried over to the display of heavy chains by the front door. The thought of freckle-faced Marcie McCleary wearing one almost made Lily laugh.

Dad's wrong on this one, she thought. *Maybe you can't always believe that small voice.*

It was a long Saturday after they got home, and Lily was more than glad when Sunday came and she could go to church.

At least I'll get to see Reni, she thought. *Then I can explain what happened.*

How she was going to do that, she wasn't quite sure. Thinking about it had been what made Saturday so long, and no little voice had shown up. She was still thinking about it in the van on the way to church.

Answer Girl ought to listen to her own advice, Dad had said. So what would I tell someone in this situation?

That had to be the way to do it. After all, she hadn't messed up yet as Answer Girl.

I'd say—tell the truth. She's your best friend. If you can't trust her, you aren't that good of friends anyway.

"Yeah," she said out loud.

Beside her, Art said, "Yeah, what?"

Joe poked her in the back from the rear seat. "You're so weird," he said.

She just hoped Reni wouldn't think that. As soon as Dad stopped the van, she hurried off to their Sunday school class and scanned the room for Reni. She was sitting on the other side, and she had Suzy next to her.

What was Suzy doing there? She didn't go to their church! Matter of fact, she didn't go to any church.

And worse, Lily worried, how was she going to explain all this to Reni with Suzy there? She had a whole other set of issues with Suzy.

There was no little voice, and it was too late to run to the bathroom. Lily sank onto a floor cushion, numbly opened her Bible, and tried to look like she was following along in 1 Corinthians as the teacher read.

Come on, Answer Girl, she thought. *Tell me what to do!*

It came to her toward the end of the lesson. She would just wait until she got home and call them separately on the phone. She'd tell Reni all about Answer Girl and why she'd gone to Ashley's instead of to her house and how she hadn't wanted to hurt Reni's feelings and that she was sorry she'd ended up doing it anyway. She'd tell Suzy that all kinds of things kept getting in the way of them talking, but she wasn't going to let that happen anymore and could they please, please meet before school tomorrow.

It felt better having a plan that didn't involve any tricks or lies and—what had Mom called it—manipulation? Going to Answer Girl must really be the ticket.

Except that after avoiding coming face-to-face with either Suzy or Reni all through church, and giving them time to get home, and then dialing Reni's number and Suzy's all afternoon, she could never get them at home. Suzy's phone just rang and rang into an apparently empty house, and Reni's dad, after telling her three different times that Reni and her mom were out, obviously turned on the answering machine.

Shoulders sagging, Lily set the phone down without leaving a message.

"It's not going well, I see."

It was Mom, standing in Lily's doorway.

"No," Lily said. "I'm trying to sort it out like Dad said."

"So you won't be grounded anymore?" Mom said.

"Not just that. I hate feeling like I've messed things up with, like, every single person I know."

"We can sure complicate our lives, can't we?" Mom said.

"You don't," Lily said. "You always know what you're supposed to do."

Mom actually laughed, and her mouth opened into a grin.

"Don't you?" Lily said.

"Not hardly. Take right now, for instance. I have absolutely no idea what to say to you."

"You don't have to say anything, Mom. I know what I did wrong."

"It didn't take a rocket scientist to figure that out. But do you know how to fix it—that's the real question."

"Yeah, only nobody's home to listen. And I feel like the longer I have to wait, the madder everybody's getting at me."

"I don't know about that. Time has been known to heal. And besides, maybe this is one of God's setups. Maybe this is giving you time to really think things through." Her mouth twitched. "Time to ask Answer Girl."

"Dad told you."

"He did. I'd like to see your work."

"You would?"

"Well, yeah—see, I'm your mom—the one who brought you into the world, potty-trained you, wiped your snotty nose—"

"I know! I just thought, since you're always so busy—"

"There will be no more of that here," Mom said. "You weren't the only one who had things to sort through." She put up her hand. "Now, I'm not excusing your behavior, but I know things like that don't just happen out of the blue. If I'd been there for you at the right moment, you might have made some different choices. I'm here for you now and from now on. Get me in a half nelson or something if you have to, but let me know when you need something. I mean it."

Lily nodded and threw her arms around Mom's neck.

I have the best parents, she thought. And then she remembered and whispered, "Thanks, God."

That helped — until Lily got to school the next morning and waited anxiously at the bench. None of the Girlz showed up, not even Kresha and Zooey. The only person she did see that she knew was Marcie McCleary, wearing the same too-big jeans she'd had on Saturday — with a heavy dog-chain thing hanging around her neck. It gave Lily a chill. She went back to thinking about the Girlz.

With visions in her head of Reni calling each of them up and telling them what a jerk Lily was, she barely managed to get through her first two classes so she could tear to the lockers before third. Nobody met her there, either. She was nauseous with nervousness by the time she did the fast-walk to Mrs. Reinhold's classroom. Reni and Suzy were standing in the hall with their backs to her. They looked like a wall that was shutting her out, but she had to break through. Swallowing back the sick feeling, Lily walked toward them. Somebody grabbed her arm from behind.

"Hey!" Ashley said when Lily turned around. "Are you okay?"

"They grounded you from the phone too?" Chelsea said. "I thought my parents were evil! Yours are the worst!"

"Bernadette sends her sympathies, by the way," Ashley said. "She said she had to threaten to run away before her parents would lighten up on her."

"Maybe you should try that," Chelsea said.

Suddenly Lily couldn't stand the sight of either pair of blue eyes that blinked at her. Life had been so much easier when they couldn't stand her.

"The bell's gonna ring," Lily said.

"I guess you gotta be careful for a while, huh?" Ashley said. "I'm sorry."

Then she stood on her tiptoes and hugged Lily's neck. Over her shoulder, Lily saw Reni and Suzy, looking right at her.

It's not like you think! Lily said with her eyes.

Reni turned away.

Lily got free of Ashley and headed for the door.

"Hey, Lily," Chelsea whispered loudly. "Don't forget."

"About what?" Lily said.

"You know." She rolled her eyes and mouthed, "Answer Girl."

"Oh. Yeah."

But that was the last thing on her mind all through Mrs. Reinhold's class, all the way to Ms. Ferringer's with Ashley and Chelsea babbling on either side of her, all through the map test. She could only focus on Suzy and Reni—and Kresha and Zooey—and try to hear a little voice inside her head.

You need to talk to them, Answer Girl told her. *You need to make them eat lunch with you and you need to tell them, even if it's all of them together. It doesn't matter who knows what anymore. They're your friends. You should have trusted them all along.*

With that decided, Lily took out a piece of paper and wrote a Lily-Gram to Reni: "Please, please, please meet me at lunch. Bring all Girlz. Need to talk to you all. Love, love, love."

While Ms. Ferringer was collecting the tests, she handed the note to Reni and watched for her reaction. Reni read it, then looked up at Lily and nodded, and turned to whisper to Suzy. Lily was waiting for her nod when Ms. Ferringer said, "Lily? Note for you."

Lily jumped. It took a full five seconds to realize Ms. Ferringer was holding out a note to her that some office aide had just brought in. It was from Mr. Miniver.

"Please come to my office as soon as the bell rings. Very important."

No! Lily wanted to shout down the hall. *I have to meet with the Girlz!*

But he was a teacher—and he said it was important. She got the sick feeling again. What if it was about the staff voting her in? What if he'd found out about it? Or what if they hadn't voted her in?

No, that couldn't be. She remembered now—Lance liked her. She'd been so busy with all the other problems, she hadn't given that one much thought. Even now she looked at Reni.

I'll meet you at lunch, I promise, she said with her eyes, and held up the note.

This time Reni's eyes answered back. She said, *Sure you will. I'll believe it when I see it.*

Believe it! Lily wanted to shout to her. *You and the Girlz mean more than any of the rest of this! Even more than Answer Girl!*

When the bell rang, she bolted from the classroom, nearly running over Ms. Ferringer's toes. She could see Mr. Miniver and still get to the cafeteria in plenty of time to talk to the Girlz. And it was more than a little voice telling her so.

Chapter 12

Mr. Miniver was waiting for Lily when she got there and ushered her into his tiny cubicle of an office just off the newspaper staff room.

"Thanks for coming right down," he said. "I have something that I think is urgent, and it's such a rush job that I'm even going over Lance's head this time."

I can SO do rush! Lily thought. She stole a look at her watch.

"I know you've already done your Answer Girl column for this time, but this just came in today's 'mail,' and I think it's such a common occurrence with you kids, and such a critical one, that we ought to pull one of the other questions and use this one instead."

He handed Lily a piece of paper with a letter typed on it.

"Sure, I'll do it tonight and give it to you tomorrow," Lily said, and she started to get up.

"Well, the thing is, you're going to have to do it right now. The paper goes to press this afternoon. Is that too much pressure?"

No! Lily wanted to say. *But let me at least go to the cafeteria first and tell my friends what's going on.*

"You're a trooper, Lily Pad," Mr. Miniver said. "Why don't you stay in here where it's quiet, and I'll keep everybody out of your hair. If you need a little time off of fifth period, I can talk to your teacher."

"No—I'll be done," Lily said, as she dug her eyes into the paper.

Dear Answer Girl,

I have a terrible problem. My parents are fighting all the time, and now they're separated. I'm afraid they're going to get a divorce, and I couldn't STAND that! I think I could talk to them and convince them how wrong they are, but I can't even get their attention. Please—you're so good at giving advice—what should I do?

—Scared

Lily picked up the first writing instrument she could find on Mr. Miniver's desk—a stubby pencil—and slid his legal pad toward her.

What would I do? Lily thought frantically. *Parent problems—come on, Answer Girl—I have to go see Reni and Suzy—*

There was no time to wait for a little voice. Lily wrote the first thing that came into her head.

Dear Scared,

I'm sorry you're going through this. If my parents were getting a divorce, I can't imagine how I'd feel.

She paused for a second. That was so true. Mom and Dad were the best. Without both of them—Lily shook her head and bent over the paper again.

You're right that you have to get their attention, and there are several ways to do that. Some people say you practically have to get them in a half nelson to make them listen to you. Others say if you change your behavior in a big way that will make them sit up and take notice. Some even say threaten to run away. The point is, do whatever it takes to get them to focus on you so you can tell them what you so need to say. Listen to that small voice in your head that guides you. You have to. This is important.

—Answer Girl

Lily was nearly in tears as she tossed the stub of a pencil onto the desk and ripped off the page. Answer Girl had gotten pretty close to home this time. She just hoped it worked on friends as well as parents.

"It's on your desk, Mr. Miniver," Lily called to him as she raced through the staff room and out the door.

There were no hall monitors to slow her down, but even so, when she reached the lunchroom, Reni, Suzy, Kresha, and Zooey were nowhere in sight. She spent the rest of the lunch period searching for them in every place she could think of. When she finally found Reni, she was already sitting in fifth-period math class, and the bell was ringing. She didn't look up, even when Lily practically stood up on her own desk and screamed at her.

"All right, let's get to work," Mr. Chester said.

Lily couldn't focus. Reni, on the other hand, seemed to be concentrating just fine. She was finished a half hour before the end of the period, handed a note to Mr. Chester, and left, presumably for the orchestra room.

Lily put her head down on her desk.

"Hey," somebody behind her said. "Lily. What's wrong?"

Lily shook her head and hoped Marcie would give up. She didn't.

"Lily," Marcie persisted. "If you feel bad, why don't you write to Answer Girl?"

Lily raised her head then and glowered at Marcie. "Shut up," she said.

She could think of nothing but Reni until she got home from school that afternoon. She called her immediately and this time she got an answer. It was Reni's mom.

"Could I speak with Reni, please?" Lily said.

"Hi, Lily," Mrs. Johnson said. "Um—Reni asked me to give you a message for her."

Lily's hopes spurted upward. "She did?"

"But I'm not going to. She has to give it to you herself. Reni?"

It sounded then as if somebody covered the mouthpiece, and there was a lot of muffled talking. Finally, Lily heard Reni's voice on the line.

"Hi," she said.

"Hi!" Lily said. She could already feel her tears coming. "I have been waiting so long to talk to you. Reni—"

"I'm glad you finally found time."

The chill in her voice stopped Lily cold.

"That's why I wanted to talk to you," Lily said slowly.

"Well, it is so too late," Reni said. "Me and Suzy—well, all us Girlz—decided if you don't have time for us and you'd rather hang around with Ashley and Chelsea and people like that, we don't have time for you either."

"But Reni, if you'll just listen—"

"Sorry. Gotta go," Reni said, and she hung up.

Lily knew it was pointless to try again. Reni had had a wall in her voice, and there was no knocking it down.

Lily thought for a moment that it might be different with Suzy or—but even as she dialed, she remembered Reni's words: me and Suzy—all the Girlz—have decided. She hung up again. Otto sniffed at her hand and licked it, but it didn't help. Not even a little. Throwing herself down on the bed, Lily started to cry. That was where Mom found her when she came home.

"Uh-oh," Mom said. She sat on the edge of the bed and gently ruffled Lily's hair. "Has Answer Girl struck out?"

"I hate Answer Girl!" Lily said.

"That's a little vicious."

"I do! I wish I'd never thought of it—ever!"

"Oh, Lil," Mom said. "I'm sorry, Hon."

And then she didn't say anything else until Lily stopped crying and sat up.

"I thought it was such a cool idea," Lily said. Mom handed her a tissue and she honked into it.

"It is a good idea," Mom said.

"No—it's the reason I'm in this mess."

"How do you figure?"

Lily shook her head. "It's too complicated."

"So, when was any mess you ever got yourself into not complicated?" Mom said, mouth twitching. "Come on—I'm halfway intelligent. Try me."

Lily sighed, and then she did try. Before she knew it, she was pouring the whole thing out for Mom, and the longer she talked, the easier it got, until Mom had to call a time-out.

"Listen," she said, "if I don't go down and cook dinner, your brothers are going to start in on three-year-old potato chips. Let me think about this some, and I promise you we'll talk more after supper. Deal?"

"I love you, Mom," Lily said.

Mom was as good as her word, and as soon as she got Joe and Art started on the dishes—with Joe proclaiming loudly that Lily was going to have to take his turn twice to make up for it—Mom and Lily slipped up to her parents' bedroom with bowls of chocolate pudding.

"I'm thinking you can't give up, Lil," Mom said. "The Girlz are hurt, especially Reni, but I think once they understand this whole thing, they'll forgive you."

"But how are they gonna understand if they won't even listen to me?"

"You're the writer. Write them letters."

"It isn't the same."

"No. Sometimes it's better." Mom's mouth twitched. "How do you think your father and I have stayed married all these years? Whenever we can't talk something out, he writes me a letter."

"Nuh-uh!"

"Cross my heart. I can be pretty pigheaded, but if I read a letter five or six times, it usually sinks in. It gives me time to really think about it. Maybe that's what Reni needs, and then she'll probably convince the other girls, don't you think?"

"It's gotta be longer than a Lily-Gram, though," Lily said.

"Excuse me?"

"Lily-Gram. That's this thing we made up where—"

"Never mind," Mom said. "Eat your pudding. I think I've absorbed all the Lily-ese I can for today."

As soon as Lily got her homework done, she started in on her letters, Reni's first. She told her all about Answer Girl and why she hadn't shared that with her and how sorry she was—and how the whole stupid column was why she went to Ashley's in the first place, only that had made things worse—and how she felt like a moron. It took her nearly two hours, and she was yawning by the time she finished but she forced herself to stay up and decorate the envelope so Reni wouldn't be able to resist opening it. She was just licking it when Mom stuck her head in.

"You don't have to write an epic novel," Mom said. "Come on, get in bed. Oh, and Lil?"

"Yeah?"

"Don't forget God. He's got to be smack in the middle of this or it's all for nothing."

"That's what Dad said. Only he also said for me to listen to the little voice in my head."

"Well, Lil—duh!" Mom's mouth twitched. "Honey, that little voice is God. You just have to shut everything else up before he'll speak. God won't compete for our attention."

"Oh," Lily said. "Duh!"

She climbed gratefully into bed and promised herself—and God—that she'd finish the other letters before school in the morning.

She did, which meant she had to catch a late ride with Mom and hurry to get to first period. After second, she stuffed the letters into the Girlz lockers because they weren't there. Then she waited.

None of them spoke to her all day or even looked her way. Ashley, Chelsea, and Bernadette, on the other hand, were in her face every chance they got.

"Did you find out yet?" Chelsea asked after fifth period.

"No," Lily said. She was trying not to sound irritated, but it was hard when she really wanted to swat all of them away like a swarm of mosquitoes. *Maybe I oughta write them letters too,* she thought.

"Why not?" Ashley said.

"Because yesterday I had to do a—I just couldn't, okay? When I find out I'll tell you."

"You don't have to get huffy about it," Chelsea said, planting her hands on her hips.

But Bernadette nudged her, and both Chelsea and Ashley plastered smiles on their faces.

"Sorry," Ashley purred. "We didn't mean to be pushy."

"I'm just anxious to find out," Chelsea said. "That's all."

Oh, yeah, I forgot, Lily thought. *You want to know who you're supposed to hate. Maybe I should just put you out of your misery and tell you it's me.*

Lily stuck a mental foot out and tripped up those thoughts to make room for one that made more sense.

Whether I tell them now or later, it doesn't matter. They're still going to hate me. I might as well get it over with.

She was even opening her mouth to say it, when the shouting started in her head again.

The whole staff's gonna be mad at you if you tell! The column will be a bust once everybody knows it's you. Even Mr. Miniver might hate you—

Lily clamped her mouth shut. The little voice had stopped trying to shout over the chaos. She wouldn't do anything until she heard it again.

The next morning dragged on the same way, and Lily felt heavy as she went from class to class, delivering bundles of the *Middle School Mirror*. She didn't even look at the "Answer Girl" column—but everybody else did.

Once again, by the time she got to lunch, that was all anybody seemed to be talking about. As she wandered through the lunchroom, hoping to see Reni and the Girlz—and maybe get a response to her letters—she heard the comments:

"It's even better this time—"

"That is so true about parents—"

"I betcha this is, like, some psychologist they hired—"

"Nobody in middle school talks like this—"

"Except you, Robbins."

Lily jerked around to see Shad Shifferdecker sitting up on a table, chewing on a toothpick, and looking at her.

"What?" she said. She could hardly hear him for the pounding in her chest.

"You talk like my shrink half the time. Buncha big words and stuff."

"I use words of more than one syllable, Shad," Lily said. "I'm sorry if that throws you."

Leo and Daniel started pummeling him with fists as they hooted and jeered, but Shad shoved them back.

"See what I mean? You talk like you're all professional or somethin'."

"Excuse me for having a brain," Lily said. She really was sick of the whole conversation, and she walked away.

"You think she's a hottie, don't you?" she heard Leo say.

"Wait'll I tell Ashley," Daniel said.

There was the sound of fists hitting skin.

Punch them a few times for me, would ya, Shad? Lily thought, as she left the lunchroom.

She got a note sixth period, but it wasn't the note she wanted from Reni. It was from Mr. Miniver:

Another winner! Keep up the good work. We're going to celebrate before school tomorrow—my treat. Get here early.

Lily had never felt less like celebrating, even that night when she showed the "Answer Girl" column to her parents. They both told her how impressed they were, and Dad insisted that the three of them go to Friendly's for sundaes.

"How come I don't get to go?" Joe said.

"It's a secret," Mom said. "Besides you've had more treats because you've won games than I can count, so I think it's Lily's turn. We'll bring you back something."

"A banana split," he said. He was still barking out his order for various toppings as Dad pulled the van out of the driveway.

It was nice to be with Mom and Dad alone and bask in the glow of all their praise. But Lily was still low when she went to bed.

God, could you please just convince the Girlz to answer me tomorrow? I don't think I can stand this any longer.

It was a heartfelt prayer—and it was answered quicker than Lily expected. Reni responded to her letter the very next morning—in a really big way.

The next morning, Lily was quietly tearing a sticky bun into little bits so the rest of the newspaper staff wouldn't realize she wasn't eating it, when the door flew open.

"This is a private party," Lance said to the intruder.

"I need to see Lily Robbins," somebody said.

Lily jerked her head up to see Reni, whose eyes were wide with something in them Lily didn't recognize. It stirred Lily's stomach to a sickening swirl.

"Can she come back later, Lily?" KJ said, swishing back her hair. "We did all this for you—"

"Quiet, Big Mouth!" Lance said to her.

"No, I cannot come back," Reni said. "I need to talk to Lily right now."

But Lily was already halfway to the door, and she didn't even fling an apology at the staff as she followed Reni out.

"How rude was that?" she heard KJ say as the door closed.

But Lily didn't care. She only had ears for Reni, no matter what she had to say.

"I'm so glad you came here," Lily said. "I've been waiting and waiting—"

"Would you just hush up for once?" Reni said. "Suzy ran away—"

"What?" Lily went cold. "That's so—not Suzy! How do you know?"

"Her mom called our house looking for her. She got up this morning, and Suzy was gone!"

"But why?" Lily said. "I don't get this—why would she run away?"

"Because you told her to."

"That's not true! I haven't even talked to Suzy since—well, a long time. I couldn't have told her that!"

"You did," Reni said. She thrust a newspaper into Lily's face. "Right here, Answer Girl."

Lily pulled her head back. "I don't understand, Reni! Honest!"

Reni snapped the paper open to Lily's column and stabbed a finger at the letter from "Scared." Lily could only stare at it.

"Suzy wrote that letter," Reni said. "And right there in your answer, you told her to run away."

"I did not!" Lily said.

She knew they were shouting at each other, and that early students could probably hear them all the way out to the front door. But all she cared about was what was happening right in front of her. She finally knew what that unfamiliar look was in Reni's eyes. It was fear.

"It says it right here," Reni said.

"But it doesn't mean go out and run away!" Lily cried. "It just means some people think that!"

"Well if you had ever actually talked to Suzy like she wanted you to," Reni said, "maybe she'd have known that and she wouldn't be missing right now!"

"I know," Lily said. She felt her face crumpling. "I'd give anything if I could go back and do it right—"

Through her tears, she could see Reni looking at her closely. "Do you really mean that?" she said.

"Of course! I know I haven't been acting like it—but, Reni, I'd do anything—anything—if I could make it right."

"Okay," Reni said. She stepped in closer, and Lily could see the tears glistening in her eyes. "Then we have to go find her."

"Absolutely," Lily said. She wiped at her nose. "I'll meet you right after school, and—"

"No," Reni said, "right now."

"But class is gonna start—"

"I thought you said you'd do anything."

"Cut school?" Lily said. "I don't know, Ren."

"Then what do we do?"

Her voice was shaky, and the tears were trailing down her face. Lily would gladly have cut every class—including Mrs. Reinhold's—if it meant making it okay for Suzy and Reni. But it didn't feel right—this idea of taking off in search of Suzy, even if it was Lily's fault that she had left home.

"I don't know yet," Lily said. "This is gonna sound weird, but I have to wait for the little voice in my head."

"What little voice?" Reni said.

"Well—God," Lily said.

Then she watched, bewildered, as Reni looked at the floor and burst into tears.

"Really—it works! My dad does it—and my mom—"

"I know!" Reni blubbered. "And I thought you always did too—only then I thought you'd forgotten how and that's why you were acting all snotty and stupid—but you still like God, don't you, Lily?"

By now, Lily was crying too. When the staff room door opened behind her, she didn't look to see who it was. She just grabbed Reni's arm.

"Come on," she whispered to her. "Let's go to the bathroom."

"Why?" Reni said.

"'Cause I can think in there."

She didn't actually do much thinking. She just helped Reni wash her face and get quiet. It was in the calm that it came to her.

"I gotta call my mom," Lily said. "She'll know what we should do."

"She's gonna tell you to let the police handle it," Reni said. "That's what my parents said. And then they made me come to school!"

"Maybe she won't say that," Lily said.

Lily really wasn't sure what her mom would say—but what she did know was that she had to go to her. No more lies. No more manipulating. No more doing anything without listening first.

She knew it was the best advice she'd given herself since Answer Girl had been born.

Lily looked at her watch. "If I hurry, I have enough time to call before the bell rings," she said.

"But I won't be able to wait 'til third period to find out what she says," Reni said.

"I'll send you a Lily-Gram."

Reni smiled for the first time that morning. "I missed you, Lily," she said.

"Me too," Lily said. And then, digging in her backpack for change, she headed for the pay phones.

"Mrs. Robbins is in class," the high school secretary told her. "May I take a message?"

"But it's important!" Lily said. "Urgent, even. This is her daughter."

"Is it an emergency?"

"Well, kind of."

"Kind of an emergency," the secretary said. Lily could hear the smirk in her voice. "How about if I take a message and get it down to her in the gym. Where can she call you back?"

"She can't," Lily said. "I'm in school. But I need to talk to her!"

"I'll tell her you called."

Lily wanted to rip the pay phone out by its cord. Instead, she nearly mowed down three kids who were waiting in line as she plowed her way through—and back to the bathroom.

The bell rang signaling the start of first period, but Lily ignored it. She shut herself in a stall and tried to get quiet. It was hard even now that she was by herself. The noise in her head was so loud that she couldn't seem to settle it down. Voices were coming from all the dark corners.

You have to DO something! they cried. *It's your fault Suzy ran away—and while you're sitting around waiting for some voice, she's getting farther and farther away! Get out of this school and start looking!*

"No!" Lily said out loud.

"No!" a voice answered back.

Lily froze. It was a good ten seconds before she realized it was her own voice echoing in the empty bathroom. But it seemed like more than that right now. It meant she was right. She had to keep listening.

I need Mom, she thought. *Or Dad.*

But it was Dad's teaching day. He'd be even harder to get in touch with than her mother. Lily's breakfast was well on its way back up before she got her mind quiet again.

"God, please," she whispered. "I need a mom or a dad. If I do this by myself, I know I'll mess it up."

Lily was crying again as she slung her backpack over her shoulder and went out into the hall. She was aware that there were people out there, but she didn't even try to hide either the tears or the stuff running out of her nose—not even when somebody touched her elbow.

"Lily Pad?" a soft voice said.

Lily looked up into Mr. Miniver's mustache.

"What's up?" he said. "I went to your first-period class to see if you were okay, and your teacher said you hadn't shown up yet."

"I'm going," Lily said, though she wasn't sure he could understand her through the sobs.

"Oh, I don't think a few minutes will matter," Mr. Miniver said. His eyes were kind—and that made Lily cry even harder. "Why don't we take a little walk 'til you calm down?" he said. "If you go to class like this, there will be nothing but questions."

"I'll get in trouble," Lily said.

"Well, you know, we teachers stick together. I'll clear it for you, how's that?"

Lily could only nod. Mr. Miniver guided her gently by the elbow toward the outside courtyard. A brisk fall breeze hit her face and magically took away some of the crying-blotches. Mr. Miniver was chuckling.

"When you weren't in your first-period class, I asked Lance when his last Lily Pad sighting was. He told me you'd just gone into the girls' restroom. I guess Lancelot keeps a pretty close eye on you."

"Oh, no!" Lily cried, and the blotches popped back onto her face.

"Okay," Mr. Miniver said. "Then I guess this isn't a boy thing. You want to tell me what's going on?"

Lily managed to look at him through her puffy eyes. He really was kind—just like Dad—and it made her want to tell him the whole stupid story.

"Do you have any kids?" she said.

"Two—a little boy and a little girl."

"Then, can you help me?" Lily said. And before he could answer, she blurted it out—probably more than he wanted or needed to know about the Girlz and her wish to be special and all the complications that tangled around Answer Girl, including the part where she'd thrown Reni's letter to the editor away. When she finally got to the part about Suzy and her letter to Answer Girl and running away, Mr. Miniver looked serious right down to his mustache.

"I just need to talk to my mom," Lily said. "It's my fault Suzy's gone, and I have to do something, only I don't know what!"

"Okay," Mr. Miniver said. "That I can help you with. Come on."

He led the way to the front office where he shooed Lily into a momentarily empty room with a phone and dialed the high school number. Within ten seconds, Lily was on hold.

"Your mom's on the way to the phone," he said. "I'll be right back."

"Do you have to go?"

"I just need to talk to some people," he said. "I won't leave you."

As the door closed and Lily clung to the receiver, she could feel the blotches ebbing away and with them the ache in her chest and the lump in her throat and the stirred-up feeling in her stomach. Still, when Mom said, "Lil?" Lily started to cry again.

"Whoa, whoa!" Mom said. "Hon, I can't understand a thing you're saying. Take some deep breaths."

Lily did.

"All right—now fill me in. The secretary said it was a 'minor emergency.' With you, there is no such thing as a 'minor' anything."

"Suzy ran away, Mom!" Lily said. "And it's my fault!"

"How do you figure?"

"You know that letter in "Answer Girl," the one about the girl with the parents who were getting a divorce?"

"Uh-huh."

"That was from Suzy—and she thought my answer meant she should run away from home!"

"Okay, refresh my memory. What was it she was supposed to accomplish by running away or doing any of the other things you put in there?"

"She needed to get her mom and dad to pay attention to her so she could tell them how wrong they are. But I didn't really mean for her to up and leave home, Mom! Honest!"

"Of course you didn't, and I don't think anyone but you would even come to that conclusion—"

"Reni did!"

"Ah." There was a short pause, and then Mom said, "I think this is a good thing, Lil."

"How could it be good? Suzy's missing!"

"Yeah, but why is she missing? She's trying to get her parents' attention. She doesn't really want to leave home permanently—she just wants to make them look for her. That tells me she can't be very far away."

"Do you really think that? You're not just saying that to calm me down?"

She could hear Mom sighing through the phone. "When are you going to learn that I don't ever say anything I don't honestly mean?"

"Oh, yeah," Lily said. She wanted to believe Mom, with every hair on her head, and that was a lot. Sitting here with her mother's voice in her ear and everything else quiet, she could almost hear a small voice saying, "Believe it. She's right."

"Where are you calling from?" Mom said.

"The office. Mr. Miniver brought me in."

"Okay—let me talk to him. You go wash your face and get yourself together. We have things to do."

Lily did just as Mom said. When she came back from the restroom, with a blotchless face and her head clear, Mr. Miniver was just hanging up.

"I need the names of the girls in your Girlz Only Group," he said to Lily. "Your mom's on her way over, and we're all going to sit down and see if we can come up with some ideas. Fair enough?"

"What about classes?" Lily said.

"All clear." Mr. Miniver's mustache was smiling again. "Sometimes there are things to learn that they don't teach in the classroom."

Before twenty minutes had passed, Mom was there in the room with Lily, and so were Reni, Zooey, and Kresha. Mr. Miniver also ushered in Reni's and Zooey's moms. Only Kresha's couldn't get away from work.

"We all have an obligation to help the Walkers find Suzy," Mom said. She looked right at Reni. "Not because Lily told her to run away in her column, but because you're her friends. You know her best, and I'm sure among the four of you, you'll be able to give us some clues. As I told Lily, she isn't far away."

Their heads all nodded solemnly.

"Now think," Mom said. "Where would she go where she would feel safe until they came looking for her?"

It got so quiet in the room, Lily was sure there must be a small voice in every person's head. She closed her eyes and tried to listen to hers.

God? she prayed. *I have been so wrong about so much stuff, and I hope you'll help me fix it. But right now, Suzy has a whole lot more problems than I do. Please help us find her. Where could she be?*

I don't even know stuff about her anymore like I used to. She said herself that everything has changed. We don't meet every day after school anymore—we're getting too big for the Clubhouse—and—

That's it. That's it!

Lily looked up at the worried, focused faces and said, "I think I know where she is."

The Girlz all started talking at once.

"Where?"

"Can we go there?"

"Are you thinking the mall? I thought of that, only—"

Mom finally silenced them with a toot on her PE whistle. Zooey looked like she was going down for a set of sit-ups.

"Okay—spill it, Lil," Mom said. "What's your idea?"

"The Clubhouse. Our old Girlz Only Clubhouse."

"No way!" Reni said. "I woulda seen her!"

"Why?" Reni's mom said. "You haven't been out there in weeks—none of you has. I was thinking of turning it into a gardening shed."

"No!" Kresha said. "It's our place!"

"But it isn't anymore," Lily said. "And Suzy talked about that. She kept saying everything was changing and she wished it wouldn't and she wished we could go back there like we used to."

"More was changing in her life than any of us knew," Zooey's mom said. "Poor little thing."

"I think you may be on to something, Lil," Mom said.

"Why don't I go home and see?" Reni's mom said. "I'll give you a call as soon as I know something."

It was the longest ten minutes in Lily's life. Although Mr. Miniver brought in sodas for all of them and assured them for the fifth time that they weren't going to be in any trouble with their teachers, the Girlz couldn't drink and they couldn't sit still. They all edged their way to Lily and clutched at each other's sweaty hands.

"This is the first time we've all been together in a really long time," Zooey said.

"All but one of us," Lily said. Her eyes were swimming again, and she probably would have started to cry if Reni hadn't squeezed her hand.

"I'm sorry about what I said, Lily," she said. "I don't think it's your fault Suzy ran away. I think it's all our faults."

"What did we do?" Zooey said, her big eyes blinking.

"I'm all busy with orchestra," Reni said. "I didn't even know she was upset 'til she called me up and asked me if I thought she should write to Answer Girl."

Kresha was nodding. "I talk about my English always. I not listen to Suzy—no, I never listen."

"Oh," Zooey said, "so you mean me making a big deal out of losing weight and buying new clothes was bad because I didn't pay any attention to Suzy?"

Mr. Miniver cleared his throat. "May I say something here? I know this is a ladies' conversation, but if I may?"

"Please do," Lily's mom said, "before they all turn on the faucets." She handed Lily a tissue.

"I don't think being interested in your own thing is necessarily bad," Mr. Miniver said. "We just all need to strike a balance between developing our own talents and showing concern for other people."

"And I'm the worst!" Lily said. "I ruined everything because of Answer Girl!"

Mr. Miniver's mustache twitched.

"I'm sorry," Lily said. "I had to tell because that's how I messed it all up."

"Tell what?" Zooey said.

"What you mean, 'Answer Girl'?" Kresha asked.

Reni shook her head at Lily. "I didn't open your letter until this morning, 'cause we all said we wouldn't ever open them. Only this morning I missed you, so I did—and that's when I knew about Answer Girl." She glanced at the Girlz. "I haven't told them."

"Told us what?" Zooey said. Her face was turning so red, her mom put her hand on her arm.

Lily looked at Mr. Miniver, and he nodded.

"I'm the Answer Girl," she said to them. "I didn't tell you because it was supposed to be a secret—and all the dumb things I did were because I wanted to keep being Answer Girl—"

"Ah, I see, " Mr. Miniver said. "Especially when it was so successful."

Mom gave Mr. Miniver one of her rare smiles. "You ought to be a counselor," she said.

"As a matter of fact, I'm finishing up my master's in counseling this semester. I'll be on the counseling staff here starting in January—"

They didn't hear the rest because just then, the phone rang. Lily jumped a foot. All four Girlz stared at Mr. Miniver as he picked it up. Lily watched his mustache.

When it tilted up at the corners, she knew, even before he gave them a thumbs-up sign. Mom had to shush the girls to keep them from squealing.

"I think that's a good idea," Mr. Miniver said into the phone. "I'll see what I can do."

Lily was practically crawling across the table when he hung up.

"You were right," he said. "Suzy's there, safe and sound—and a little hungry. Her mom and dad are on their way, but Reni's mom suggested that it might be good for Suzy to talk to Lily. It seems she still has some confusion about a few things."

Lily's chest immediately started to ache. "I don't know," she said. "So far my advice hasn't been too good. I don't think I'm such a good Answer Girl anymore."

Mom reached over and put her hand on Lily's shoulder. "You don't have to be Answer Girl to help your friend," she said. "Just tell her what you know is true. Let her know you love her."

"I wish you could go with me," Lily said, "but I know you have to go back to school."

"Lil," her mom said, "wild horses couldn't keep me from going with you."

They got to the Johnsons before Suzy's parents did, but even that quick trip gave Lily enough time to work up a lump in her throat and a pair of sweaty palms.

When her mom turned off the ignition in the van, Lily said, "I'm scared. What if Suzy hates me now?"

"That would be a bummer," Mom said. "I think we ought to pray."

So they did. Mom asked God to please whisper in Lily's ear so she would know what to say, to fill her heart with love so she'd know what to do, and to strengthen her mind with honesty so she'd know just who to be.

Lily was still nervous, but she knew now she could at least get out of the car. Just as she opened the door, Mom said, "Lil—I hope you know that you already are special. You don't have to prove that to anybody."

Lily nodded, but she didn't feel particularly special as she crossed Reni's yard to the Clubhouse. She felt like a girl who'd made some big mistakes and wanted more than anything to fix them.

The Clubhouse door was closed, and Lily peeked in the tiny window before she opened it. Suzy was in there all right, sitting on a hot-pink cushion, toying with one of Reni's mom's brownies but not eating it. Her dark hair was, as always, shiny and neat, but her face was red and swollen from crying. She looked small and alone.

But you're not alone, Suzy.

It was a small voice in Lily's head. She opened the door and said, "Hi, Suzy. Want some company?"

Suzy looked up from the brownie and for an awful moment, her eyes didn't even seem to see Lily. They just stared vacantly, as if she didn't recognize her.

Lily fought back the tears. *She has a right to hate me, but I have to help her anyway. I have to show her I'm still her friend.*

The awful moment passed, and Suzy broke into a puffy smile.

"Lily!" she said. "You came!"

"It took me long enough," Lily said. "I'm sorry I didn't make time for you before—"

"You were busy—"

"But I shouldn't have been too busy for you."

"It's okay, though. I got advice from Answer Girl, and it worked! Mrs. Johnson said my parents are on their way over here—both of them, Lily!"

Lily shook her head until her red hair was all over her face. Brushing it back with impatient fingers, she sat down next to Suzy.

"Brownie?" Suzy asked politely.

"No! Suzy—listen to me! Answer Girl was wrong!"

"No, she wasn't. See, she said some people get their parents to listen by doing all these different things and when none of the rest of them worked for me, I tried this, and—"

"No! That's wrong! Suzy—I'm Answer Girl."

Suzy blinked. "You, Lily?"

"Yeah—and I got a big head about it and thought I was all that because everybody went nuts over it—but I shoulda been more careful how I said that stuff in my answer to you. Bernadette was the one who said she threatened to run away when her parents wouldn't listen to her. I shouldn't ever have put that in there!"

"But it worked," Suzy said again.

"We coulda thought of something better," Lily said. "If only I'd been there when you wanted to talk to me! If only I'd guessed it was you calling me on the phone all the time and then hanging up. It was, wasn't it?"

Suzy nodded. "I wanted to talk to you in person."

"And from now on, you'll always be able to. I promise."

Just then Lily heard voices in the yard, coming closer to the Clubhouse. Suzy heard them too because she cocked her head, her eyes gleaming, even in the dimness.

"I don't know whether to hug her or smack her," a man's voice said.

"Don't you dare smack her!" said a woman's. "That's the whole problem with this family—you're too hard on the girls and on me!"

"For once could you think about something besides yourself? It's your selfishness that's the problem. I'm just trying to have some order in my own house. If it were left up to you, chaos would run the place instead of me!"

Lily swallowed hard and looked at Suzy. She had both hands over her face, and her shoulders were shaking.

"Help me hide, Lily!" she whispered. "If you're my friend, help me hide. It's just gonna be the same if I go back—"

Lily's thoughts scrambled in her head as she looked frantically around the tiny clubhouse. There was certainly no place to hide in here where even a blind person couldn't find her. She might be able to stall them until—

And then the thoughts stopped. Lily took a deep breath and waited until they all went back to their dark corners. Then she listened.

There was a tap on the door.

"Lily! Do something!" Suzy's whisper was high-pitched with panic, but Lily brought her face close and whispered back, "You can't run away, Suzy. You have to go home with them."

"It's awful at home!"

"Then come to my house anytime you want to."

Where that idea had come from, Lily didn't know. She only knew that it stopped Suzy's tears and got her to crawl to the door and open it to her parents. When nobody smacked her, Lily slipped past them and ran to her mom.

"Good job, Answer Girl," Mom said.

But Lily shook her head as she buried it in Mom's chest. "I'm through being Answer Girl, Mom."

"I'm liking that. On one condition."

Lily looked up at her. "What?" she said.

"That you keep listening to Answer Man instead." Her mouth twitched at the corners, and she pointed up.

"Oh, yeah," Lily said. And then she climbed into the van and had her last good cry.

The next few weeks had more ups and downs than a yo-yo.

Mom and Dad talked Suzy's parents into getting counseling and advised them to let Suzy see Mr. Miniver a few times a week. That was an "up." So was Suzy coming over to Lily's when things got ugly at her house.

But Lily's session with Mr. M. and the newspaper staff was a definite "down." She told them that she'd had to give away the secret to her best friends, practically to save the life of one of them, though she was sure none of them would tell a soul. But that didn't matter, she told them, because she didn't want to be Answer Girl anymore anyway—not unless she could turn the column into "Answer Man" and tell people how to listen to God's voice in their heads.

"And Mr. Miniver already told me he doesn't think the school board would approve of that," she said as she finished, "since we're not supposed to talk about our religious beliefs in places like the school newspaper. So I guess somebody else'll have to take over."

"Nobody else can do it!" Doug said. His big eyebrow was wrinkled like a caterpillar. He genuinely looked sad, and it made Lily wonder if somebody so nice could actually like Bernadette.

There was general agreement with Doug from everybody except Lance, who was back to curling his lip, Adamson style.

"I just don't get why you can't do it," KJ said to Lily. "Even if your friends do tell—everybody thinks you're the new Dr. Laura or something—what difference does it make that you're a seventh grader?"

"Big difference," Lance said. "Look at the way this turned out. An eighth grader wouldn't have let this happen. It's all about how mature you are."

"Oh, I don't know—" Mr. Miniver started to say.

But Lily held her hands up in a time-out signal, the way her mom always did. "He's right," she said. "I wasn't ready for it. I think I'll just correct people's spelling for a while." She looked at Lance, "Even if you make life miserable for me."

"What's that about?" Mr. Miniver asked.

Lily sat back and let Lance try to explain it. That was an "up." And so was the fact that, according to Ashley, Lance said Lily was no longer cool.

"That means he doesn't like you as a girlfriend anymore," she explained to Lily.

"That's breakin' my heart," Lily said.

That brought on enough eye-rolling from Ashley and Chelsea to last Lily through the rest of adolescence. Bernadette, however, didn't see it their way. From what Lily could observe, she broke off all ties with her two former friends and started her own group.

"We're gonna be ten times more popular than Ashley and Chelsea and their loser boyfriends ever were," she told Lily. "You oughta join us."

Lily laughed. She didn't even have to put on an act to say, "I don't think so, Bernadette."

"Look, we're not gonna be like them," Bernadette said, although she rolled her eyes exactly the way they did. "They totally used you to try to find out who Lance liked. My group isn't gonna do stuff like that."

"Mine won't either," Lily said. "I think I'll stay where I am."

It was definitely an "up" that the Girlz met every day before school and at lunch and at least once a week after school in Zooey's basement. The Clubhouse really was too small, and after seeing the Girlz in action the day Suzy ran away, Zooey's mom wanted to do something for them. At their first meeting, Zooey said the basement had never looked so good. Kresha said it was nice to be able to stand up straight.

Whenever they weren't together, they were sending each other Lily-Grams—only Lily asked them to change the name to Girlz-Grams.

"It isn't all about me all the time," she said. And then she had to quiet her mind. Remembering how she'd made it all about her was a "down."

However, when Lily took stock at the end of each day with Otto and China and her journal and God, the "ups" always won out over the "downs." In fact, one thing she thought was going to be a "down" even turned out to be an "up."

Mr. Miniver and the office cleared Lily's absence from first, second, and third periods on Runaway Day, and two of her teachers gave her makeup work without comment. Mrs. Reinhold, however, asked Lily to come in after school for a "chat."

"What do you think she'll do to you?" Zooey said at lunch. Her eyes were so wide and frightened that you'd have thought she was the one facing a conference with "Stranglehold."

"She won't do nothing to Lily!" Kresha said.

"Anything," Suzy whispered to her.

"You don't know her," Reni said. "She's pretty mean. She already called Lily's mom just because she wasn't in her seat three times when the bell rang—and two of those weren't even her fault!"

"Thanks for reminding me, Reni," Lily said. "This is really making me feel better."

"We ought to pray," Suzy said. They all stared at her. "Well, that's what they tell you in church. I only went that one time, but that's what they said, didn't they?"

So the Girlz did pray, right there at lunch. There was a chorus of hoots and hollers from Shad Shifferdecker's table, but the Girlz ignored them. With so many other things to think about, that was getting easier and easier to do. And that was an "up" if Lily had ever seen one.

The rest of the afternoon, whenever Lily felt her stomach getting stirred up over the "chat" with Mrs. Reinhold, she remembered the Girlz praying with her. And then she remembered to listen for Answer Man. By the time her last class was over, she was practically wringing out her palms, but at least she didn't feel like throwing up.

Mrs. Reinhold was behind her desk as usual when Lily arrived, but she got up and moved to a student's chair, motioning for Lily to join her. Lily wiped her hands on her jeans and sat down.

Just tell her the truth, Lily reminded herself.

But Mrs. Reinhold didn't give her a chance. An explanation wasn't what she had in mind at all.

"I went straight to Mr. Miniver when you missed my class," Mrs. Reinhold said, "thinking he had taken you out for something to do with the newspaper. I don't approve of extracurricular activities interfering with academics." She folded her spider-veined hands on the desktop. "He told me what it was about, probably more than your privacy should allow. I hope you don't mind my knowing about your personal business."

Lily shook her head.

"What I want to say to you—"

Here it comes, Lily thought. *Stay calm—listen.* "—is that I admire the turnaround you've made since our last chat. You obviously paid careful attention when I told you to be careful whom you chose to spend your time with. In fact, if I had known the type of student involved with the newspaper, I would never have put you in that position. Although—" Lily thought she saw the trace of a smile on Mrs. Reinhold's stiff lips, "according to Mr. Miniver, you've more than held your own with that group."

She paused, and Lily thought she should say something.

"What about my makeup work?" she said. "I don't want to get behind."

"What you were doing was much more important," Mrs. Reinhold said. "I won't count that day's assignment against you, although judging from your column, you need a little work on commas. Review that section in the grammar book before you write your next Answer Girl."

"He told you that too, huh?"

Mrs. Reinhold shook her head. "He didn't have to tell me. I recognized your writing style in the first issue."

"Nuh-uh!" Lily said, and then she covered her mouth. "I mean—how could you?"

This time, Mrs. Reinhold really did smile, and it changed her whole face. Her eyes out-twinkled Mr. Miniver's.

"Lilianna," she said, "you are one of a kind—that's how."

When she left the classroom that day, Lily felt that for once, maybe she was—thanks to the Answer Man.

Check out this excerpt from the next book in the Lily Series!

Lily the Rebel

zonderkidz

Chapter 1

So I say, 'Okay, we gotta get this done or Mr. Nutting's gonna give us all zeroes,' and Benjamin says, 'Who cares?' Then I say, 'I do! I've got an A in this class, and I wanna keep it,' and he's, like, 'Wow, big deal, man, an A—dude.' You know, he's acting all smart—and then the minute, I mean the *minute* Mr. Nutting looks over at us, Benjamin starts acting all perfect, like he's this little angel or something. I so wanted to gag. I mean, he's like, *so* fake. You oughta be glad he wasn't in your study group."

Lily took a breath and switched the phone to her left ear. On the other end of the line, her best friend Reni waited patiently. She knew, of course, that there was much more.

"Anyway," Lily went on, "I don't think kids who act all hypocritical like that deserve to be in accelerated classes. It's worse than if Shad Shifferdecker was in there."

"Uh, no," Reni said. "*Nothing* is worse than having Shad Shifferdecker in your class—especially a science class, with all those chemicals and stuff. What he couldn't do when Mr. Nutting's back was turned!"

"Shad doesn't bother me that much anymore, 'cause at least he admits that he thinks school is a total waste of time. What *bothers* me are boys like Benjamin who make the teachers think they're, like, these scholars, and then the rest of the time they get away with everything they can." Lily rearranged herself on the bed. "Oh—do you know what he did Monday when you weren't there?"

"No, tell me!"

"Okay—we're all taking this pop quiz, okay, and—"

"Lil—you're *still* on that phone?"

Lily stopped just short of propping her feet up on the wall and looked at her mom, who was standing in Lily's bedroom doorway with her gym bag in her hand.

Lily covered the mouthpiece with her hand. "I just got on," she said.

"Yeah—before I left for the gym—an hour and a half ago."

Only then did Lily notice that her mom's usually neat golden-brown ponytail was halfway out of its scrunchie and her cheeks were about the color of Pepto-Bismol.

"Oh," Lily said. "You already went?"

"Went. Worked out. Stopped at the gas station—the post office." Mom nodded toward the phone. "Your time's more than up. Say adios."

"Okay," Lily said, mane of red hair scattering as she nodded, "just let me finish telling Reni this one thing."

"I know your 'one things', Lil," Mom said. "Save it for the next marathon conversation."

"Do you need to make a call or something?" Lily said.

Mom squinted her doe-brown eyes a little—a sure sign that she was getting annoyed. "No," she said. "I just need for you to follow the rule. Thirty minutes."

"Art was on here for two hours last night!"

"Remind me to have him hanged at sunrise. Meanwhile—"

Mom made a cutting motion across her throat, and as she disappeared from the doorway, Lily sighed.

"I gotta go," she said into the phone.

"Did you go over time?" Reni said.

"Yeah. And I was just getting to the good part!"

"We can finish up tomorrow morning."

"You know what? When I get older and have my own place, I am *so* gonna talk as long as I want. I want one of those phones that—"

"Lilianna!"

"See ya," Reni said.

Lily hurriedly poked the off button on the cordless phone. When Mom started calling her Lilianna, it was time to snap to. Lily rubbed at the prickly feeling crawling up the back of her neck and looked down at her gray mutt, Otto, who was asleep on his back on the floor, all four paws in the air.

"If I had hackles like you," Lily said, "they'd be standing up right now."

She propped her long, lanky legs up on the wall and looked longingly at the phone.

I remember when I'd rather play word games with Dad than talk on the phone anytime, she thought. She ran her fingers over the receiver. *I used to wonder what people found to talk about for so long. Now I could talk to the Girlz all day and still not get it all in.*

"There's the phone. Dude, I've been looking all over for it."

Lily's brother Art sauntered into her room, blue eyes looking hungrily at the cordless phone. He was tall and lean like Lily, but at sixteen, he had the whole lanky thing more under control. He snatched up the phone and flipped it deftly from one hand to the other, high over his short, red hair.

"The rule is you're supposed to put it back on the hall table when you're done," he said, "so the next person doesn't have to go looking for it."

"Then how come I had to dig under your bed for it when I wanted to use it?" Lily said.

"Otto musta dragged it under there. How ya doin', Muttsky?"

Otto lifted his wiry head and growled out of the side of his mouth. Art grinned.

"Thanks, pal. I was starting to think you didn't love me anymore."

"Speaking of love," Lily said, nodding toward the phone, "are you gonna call Traci?"

"Traci? Nah, we broke up a long time ago."

"You just went out with her Friday night!"

"Oh. I guess time flies when you're having fun." He stopped juggling the receiver and narrowed his eyes at her. "Since when did you start keeping track of my love life?"

"Since you started hogging the phone all the time!"

"Like that makes a difference. We only get a half hour at a time anyway." His wide mouth went into a grin. "I just string my half hours all together."

"Get out," Lily said cheerfully.

He did, but her younger brother Joe appeared less than ten seconds later and tried to play the "Wipe Out" drum solo on the doorframe.

"What?" Lily said.

"Mom says to come down and set the table."

"It can't be my turn again!"

"It's right on the chart—U-G-L-Y. That's you, right?"

"Get out," Lily said—and this time not cheerfully.

"Don't do it, then," he said as he went off down the hall. "Get in trouble. See if I care."

Was I that obnoxious when I was nine? she wondered.

Once again she put her hand up to the prickly place on the back of her neck as she dragged herself down to the kitchen.

No, she thought, digging through the silverware drawer for at least two forks that matched. *When I was nine, I was all into putting on plays in the backyard and going through the trunks in the attic for dress-up stuff and wishing I was Jo in* Little Women.

The thought of it made her snicker. She had definitely changed. Now she was twelve—in the second month of seventh grade—spending most of her time doing homework and talking on the phone … when she was allowed to.

"We need to put soup spoons on," Mom said. "Harriet sent me home with enough homemade vegetable soup for all of us." Her mouth twitched in that way that took the place of a smile. "None of us are going to get homemade soup any other way, that's for sure. I was hoping cooking would become one of your things, Lil. Then we might get some decent meals around here."

"What 'things'?" Lily said.

"Last month you were going to be the next Dear Abby. Last summer it was Martha Stewart. In May, you had—"

"Okay, I get it," Lily said. She dealt the plates onto the place mats, scowling. "They aren't 'things.' I was just trying to figure out what I wanted to do, that's all."

"*Was*?" Mom said. "Past tense?"

"Yeah."

"So you're, like, *so* over that?"

Her mouth was twitching at both corners, but Lily didn't find it the least bit amusing. She could feel the scowl getting deeper and the prickles getting pricklier.

"Could you please not make fun of the way I talk?" she said. "And that was just a phase I was going through. I know who I am now."

"I see."

"I'm *so* serious!"

Mom turned from the pot she was stirring on the stove and wiped her hands on the seat of her sweats. "I *so* know. Okay—sorry—no more teasing."

Good, Lily thought.

"Can I just ask you this, though?"

"Sure."

"Is it now safe to pack away your modeling portfolio, your first-aid kit—"

Lily didn't holler "Mo-om!" this time. She knew it was going to come out with an edge that would bring on the "Lily, don't take that tone with me." Instead, she said, through her teeth, "I'm going out to the laundry room to get some more napkins."

She found them right away, but she hiked herself up onto the top of the dryer and sat there for a few minutes, hugging the package of napkins to her chest. If she went back to the kitchen right now, she wasn't sure she could keep herself from hissing like a copperhead at everything Mom said.

This is so weird, she thought. *Just a couple of weeks ago, Mom and Dad were so cool. Now all of a sudden, it's like they're in my face all the time. It's driving me nuts!*

That, she knew, was why it was so much fun to talk to Reni and the other "Girlz"—Suzy, Zooey, and Kresha—on the phone.

Without them, Lily thought, *I'd go bonkers.*

"Where'd you go for those napkins, Lil?" Mom called from the kitchen. "Ireland?"

Lily sighed and slid off the dryer. She might just go bonkers anyway.

She thought about it some more that night when she was curled up with her Bible, her journal, China (her giant stuffed Panda), and Otto. That was the usual setup for her quiet time with God.

"So, God," she wrote in her journal, "I know I'm supposed to get my mind all silent so I can hear you do that quiet-voice thing in there—but how am I supposed to get it to be still when everybody else is always *at* me?"

She closed her eyes and waited. Nothing came up except her hackles.

Then, God, could you please help me find a way to stop this prickling in my neck? It makes me act so cranky around here!

Home wasn't the only place where she wanted to tear out handfuls of her wild, red hair. Middle school, she decided the next morning, was enough to make her bald by the end of the semester.

That day, it started when she and the Girlz—except for Kresha—were gathered on their usual bench before first period, eating the Nutri-Grain bars Zooey had brought for all of them. They were being careful to put their wrappers in the trash can lest "Deputy Dog" pounce on them. She was the school cop who monitored the halls before and after school and between classes. Eighth graders said she went easy on people the first month of school, but right about now, she usually started writing people up right and left.

"What—no donuts?" Reni asked, as she peered into the grocery bag. "No cinnamon buns?"

"I don't eat that kind of stuff anymore," Zooey said. "Since I started losing all my baby fat from doing aerobics in PE, I figure why blimp back up again?"

"You were never fat," Suzy said. She tilted her head so that her silky-black bob of hair fanned across her cheek. "You were just ... fluffy."

"Nah," Reni said, "she was fat—"

"Hey," Lily said quickly, "anybody know where Kresha is?"

"She had to go see her ESL teacher," Suzy said.

"Why?" Zooey asked, hazel eyes round. "She's doing great with her English now." Kresha was from Croatia and had recently experienced a learning spurt that was making her sound more American by the hour.

"Ask her," Reni said.

She nodded toward the stairs where a flush-faced Kresha was leaping down the "up" steps two at a time. Her wispy, sand-colored hair looked even more disheveled than usual, and her backpack was flying out behind her.

"Girl-za!" she shouted at them. "I have the good news!"

"And I have *bad* news."

All five heads turned to see Deputy Dog strolling out from under the staircase, thumbs hooked into her uniform belt. Her eyes were on Kresha, and as far as Lily could tell, she was practically licking her chops.

Kresha's excited grin didn't fade as she smacked her bangs away from her eyebrows and said, "I sorry. No yelling in the halls, right, sir?"

Reni grabbed on to Lily's arm, and Lily cringed. Zooey and Suzy looked as if they were both about to pass out.

Deputy Dog drew herself up out of her belt to full stature and glared at Kresha. "Contrary to popular belief," she said, "I am not a guy, so you can drop the sir."

Kresha shrugged happily and kept grinning as she edged toward the Girlz. "Okay," she said. "I never do it again."

"Excuse me?"

"I don't think she understood you," Suzy said to the officer. Her voice was jittery. Suzy seldom spoke up around adults, even when she *really* had to be excused to the restroom or something.

Deputy Dog looked at Suzy. "Was I talking to you, Missy?" she said.

Lily could see Suzy freezing right to the spot. Her face went so white that her dark eyes stood out like two buttons of fear. The prickles went up the back of Lily's neck.

"Was I?" the woman said.

Suzy shook her head.

"I can't hear your brains rattling in there. How about an answer?"

Leave her alone! Lily wanted to shout. *Can't you see she's scared to death?*

"No," Suzy said finally—in a voice frail as a spiderweb.

Deputy Dog looked as if she wanted to say more to Suzy, but Kresha raised her hand, as if she were in class.

Oh, no, Lily thought. *Kresha—not now!*

But Deputy Dog said, "I'll ask the questions. Put your hand down."

"I will not yell again," Kresha said. "I promise."

"Yeah, well, yelling's the least of your problems, Missy. Are you aware that you just came down the 'up' staircase—and at a dead run, no less?"

"It wasn't exactly a run," Reni muttered to Lily out of the side of her mouth.

"Do you know the rules in this school, Missy?" Deputy Dog said. "Or don't they print them in your language?"

"I know rules," Kresha said. Her eyes looked confused, but she was still smiling.

"Then am I to assume that you have no respect for them—like your friends here?"

The Girlz looked at each other, wide-eyed. Zooey, Lily saw, was close to tears, and Suzy was already sniffling.

"What did *we* do?" Reni said.

Deputy Dog reached behind Zooey's back and snatched away the grocery bag. "Eating in the halls," she said.

Lily cleared her throat. "Um—we didn't know we weren't supposed to eat. I don't think that's in the rules." She wanted to add, *Of course there's so many of them, who can remember them all?*

"We didn't throw our wrappers on the ground," Zooey said, voice teetering.

"Bully for you," Deputy Dog said. "I'll arrange for medals for all of you." She folded the top of the grocery bag and tossed the whole thing into the trash can. "No eating except in the cafeteria," she said. She pulled a pad out of her back pocket and a pencil from behind her ear. "Names," she said.

Suzy gave a full-out whimper, and Zooey let the floodgates go and started bawling. Deputy Dog drew up her mouth in disgust.

"Don't try that with me," she said. "I've seen enough tears to drown a litter of kittens, and it never works. Dry up and give me your names."

"Reni Johnson—"

"Kresha Ragina—"

Lily put one arm around Zooey and one around Suzy, which left no hands for trying to smooth down the porcupine quills that were poking at her whole spine. *This is so not fair!* she wanted to scream. *Why don't you go find Shad Shifferdecker and haul him in—he must be doing something wrong—but leave us alone!*

"So are you going to tell me your name or are you planning to wait for your lawyer?"

Lily realized with a jerk that Deputy Dog was talking to her. The prickles turned inward and stabbed at her stomach.

"Lily Robbins," she said. "But—what's this for?"

"This little missy," she said, jabbing her chin toward Kresha, "is getting after-school detention for misbehaving in the halls. The rest of you are getting written warnings about food consumption in non-designated areas. Except you."

Her eyes—a muddy shade of brown—pierced into Lily's.

"Me?" Lily said.

"That's who I'm looking at. You are getting a referral to the counselor. The two of you need to talk about your bad attitude."

Lily and the Creep (Book Three)
Softcover • ISBN-10: 0-310-23252-X
ISBN-13: 978-0-310-23252-0
Lily learns what it means to be a child of God and how to develop God's image in herself.

The Buddy Book
Softcover • ISBN-10: 0-310-70064-7
ISBN-13: 978-0-310-70064-7
(Companion Nonfiction to *Lily and the Creep*)
The Buddy Book is all about relationships—why they're important, how lousy your life can be if they're crummy, what makes a good one, and how God is the Counselor for all of them.

Lily's Ultimate Party (Book Four)
Softcover • ISBN-10: 0-310-23253-8
ISBN-13: 978-0-310-23253-7
After Lily's plans for the "ultimate" party fall apart, her grandmother shows Lily that having a party for the right reasons will help to make it a success.

The Best Bash Book
Softcover • ISBN-10: 0-310-70065-5
ISBN-13: 978-0-310-70065-4
(Companion Nonfiction to *Lily's Ultimate Party*)
The Best Bash Book provides fun party ideas and alternatives, as well as etiquette for hosting and attending parties.

Ask Lily (Book Five)
Softcover • ISBN-10: 0-310-23254-6
ISBN-13: 978-0-310-23254-4
Lily becomes the "Answer Girl" and gives anonymous advice in the school newspaper.

The Blurry Rules Book
Softcover • ISBN-10: 0-310-70152-X
ISBN-13: 978-0-310-70152-1
(Companion Nonfiction to *Ask Lily*)
Explaining ethics for an 8-12 year old girl! You will discover that although there may not always be an easy answer or a concrete rule, there's always a God answer.

Available now at your local bookstore!

zonder**kidz**

Lily the Rebel (Book Six)

Softcover • ISBN-10: 0-310-23255-4
ISBN-13: 978-0-310-23255-1

Lily starts to question the rules at home and at school and decides she may not want to follow the rules.

The It's MY Life Book

Softcover • ISBN-10: 0-310-70153-8
ISBN-13: 978-0-310-70153-8
(Companion Nonfiction to *Lily the Rebel*)

The It's MY Life Book is designed to help you find balance in your struggle for independence, so you can become not only your best self, but most of all your God-intended self.

Lights, Action, Lily! (Book Seven)

Softcover • ISBN-10: 0-310-70249-6
ISBN-13: 978-0-310-70249-8

Cast in a Shakespearean play at school by a mere fluke, Lily is immediately convinced she's destined for a career on Broadway, but finally learns through a series of entanglements that relationships are more important than a perfect performance.

The Creativity Book

Softcover • ISBN-10: 0-310-70247-X
ISBN-13: 978-0-310-70247-4
(Companion Nonfiction to *Lights, Action, Lily!*)

Discover your creativity and learn to enjoy the arts in this fun, activity-filled book written by Nancy Rue.

Lily Rules! (Book Eight)

Softcover • ISBN-10: 0-310-70250-X
ISBN-13: 978-0-310-70250-4

Lily is voted class president at her school, but unlike her predecessors who have been content to sail along with the title and a picture in the yearbook, Lily is out to make changes.

The Uniquely Me Book

Softcover • ISBN- 10: 0-310-70248-8
ISBN- 13: 978-0-310-70248-1
(Companion Nonfiction to *Lily Rules!*)

At some point, every girl wonders why she was born and why she's the way she is. Well, author Nancy Rue has written the perfect book designed to answer all those nagging uncertainties from a biblical perspective.

Available now at your local bookstore!

zonder**kidz**

Rough & Rugged Lily (Book Nine)

Softcover • ISBN-10: 0-310-70260-7
ISBN-13: 978-0-310-70260-3

Lily's convinced she's destined to become a great outdoorswoman, but when the Robbins family is stranded in a snowstorm on the way to a mountain cabin to celebrate Christmas, she learns the real meaning of survival and how dependent she is on the material things of life.

The Year 'Round Holiday Book

Softcover • ISBN-10: 0-310-70256-9
ISBN-13: 978-0-310-70256-6
(Companion Nonfiction to *Rough and Rugged Lily*)

The Year 'Round Holiday Book will help you celebrate traditional holidays with not only fun and pizzazz, but with deeper meaning as well.

Lily Speaks! (Book Ten)

Softcover • ISBN-10: 0-310-70262-3
ISBN-13: 978-0-310-70262-7

Lily enters the big speech contest at school and learns the up and downsides of competition through her pain and disappointment, as well as the surprise benefits, and how God heals jealousy, envy, and self-doubt.

The Values & Virtues Book

Softcover • ISBN-10: 0-310-70257-7
ISBN-13: 978-0-310-70257-3
(Companion Nonfiction to *Lily Speaks!*)

The Values & Virtues Book offers you tips and skills for improving your study habits, sportsmanship, relationships, and every area of your life.

Available now at your local bookstore!

zonder**kidz**

Horse Crazy Lily (Book Eleven)

Softcover • ISBN-10: 0-310-70263-1
ISBN-13: 978-0-310-70263-4

Lily's in love! With horses?! Back in the "saddle" for another exciting adventure, Lily's gone western and feels she's destined to be the next famous cowgirl.

The Fun-Finder Book

Softcover • ISBN-10: 0-310-70258-5
ISBN-13: 978-0-310-70258-0
(Companion Nonfiction to *Horse Crazy Lily*)

The Fun-Finder Book is designed to help you find out what you like so that you can develop your own just-for-you hobby. And if you just can't figure it out, a self-quiz helps you recognize your likes and dislikes as you discover your God-given talent.

Lily's Church Camp Adventure (Book Twelve)

Softcover • ISBN-10: 0-310-70264-X
ISBN-13: 978-0-310-70264-1

Lily learns a real lesson about the essential habits of the heart when she and the Girlz attend Camp Galilee.

The Walk-the-Walk Book

Softcover • ISBN-10: 0-310-70259-3
ISBN-13: 978-0-310-70259-7
(Companion Nonfiction to *Lily's Church Camp Adventure*)

Every young girl needs the training that develops positive and lifelong spiritual habits. Prayer, Bible study, devotion, simplicity, confession, worship, and celebration are foundational spiritual disciplines to help you "walk-the-walk."

Lily's in London?! (Book Thirteen)

Softcover • ISBN-10: 0-310-70554-1
ISBN-13: 978-0-310-70554-3

Lily's London adventures strengthen her relationship with God as she realizes, more than ever, there are many possibilities for walking her spiritual path in Christ.

Lily's Passport to Paris (Book Fourteen)

Softcover • ISBN-10: 0-310-70555-X
ISBN-13: 978-0-310-70555-0

Lily visits Paris and meets Christophe, an orphan boy at the mission where her mom is working. While helping Christophe to understand who God is, Lily finally discovers her own mission. This last book in the series also includes a letter from Nancy Rue, which tells what happens to the characters after the series ends, and introduces the character of Sophie LaCroix from the Faithgirlz! Sophie Series.

Available now at your local bookstore!

zonder**kidz**

NIV Young Women of Faith Bible

General Editor: Susie Shellenberger

Hardcover • ISBN-10: 0-310-91394-2
ISBN-13: 978-0-310-91394-8

Softcover • ISBN-10: 0-310-70278-X
ISBN-13: 978-0-310-70278-8

Now there is a study Bible designed especially for girls ages 8 to 12. Created to develop a habit of studying God's Word in young girls, the *NIV Young Women of Faith Bible* is full of cool, fun to read in-text features that are not only interesting, but provide insight. It has 52 weekly studies thematically tied to the *NIV Women of Faith Study Bible* to encourage a special time of study for mothers and daughters to share in God's Word.

Available now at your local bookstore!

zonder**kidz**

zonderkidz.

We want to hear from you. Please send your comments
about this book to us in care of zreview@zondervan.com. Thank you.

Grand Rapids, MI 49530
www.zonderkidz.com